THE HUNDRED
AND NINETY-NINE
STEPS

The Hundred and Ninety-Nine Steps

Michel Faber

CANONGATE

First published in Great Britain in 2001 by
Canongate Books Ltd, 14 High Street, Edinburgh EH1 1TE.
Paperback edition published in 2002.

1 3 5 7 9 10 8 6 4 2

Copyright © Michel Faber, 2001
The moral right of the author has been asserted.

British Library Cataloguing-in-Publication Data
A catalogue record for this book is available on
request from the British Library

ISBN 1 84195 328 8

Designed by Jim Hutcheson

Typeset by Patty Rennie Production, Glenbervie
in 12.4/16pt Mrs Eaves
Printed and bound by WS Bookwell, Finland

www.canongate.net

So word by word, and line by line,
The dead man touch'd me from the past . . .

Tennyson, 'In Memoriam'

Acknowledgements

THIS BOOK EXISTS BECAUSE Keith Wilson, Artist in Residence at Whitby Abbey during summer 2000, asked me to come and write a short story inspired by the English Heritage dig. My thanks to him for this, and for his guided tours of Whitby when Eva and I were there.

A number of folk were generous with their time and expertise in advising me on details of fact. Any errors that remain are therefore due to my fault, my fault, my grievous fault, and should not be blamed on English Heritage, Cath Buxton (archaeologist), Stephen and Pam Allen (paper conservators), Carla Graham, Colin Manlove or the Whitby Literary & Philosophical Society. I also acknowledge the valuable work of Father Roland Connelly and historian Andrew White. As always, Eva Youren offered wise advice and felicitous ideas.

No animals were harmed or coerced in the making of this story.

Michel Faber
February 2001

THE HAND CARESSING HER CHEEK was gentle but disquietingly large — as big as her whole head, it seemed. She sensed that if she dared open her lips to cry out, the hand would cease stroking her face and clasp its massive fingers over her mouth.

'Just let it happen,' his voice murmured, hot, in her ear. 'It's going to happen anyway. There's no point resisting.'

She'd heard those words before, should have known what was in store for her, but somehow her memory had been erased since the last time he'd held her in his arms. She closed her eyes, longing to trust him, longing to rest her head in the pillowy crook of his arm, but at the last instant, she glimpsed sideways, and saw the knife in his other hand. Her scream was gagged by the blade slicing deep into her throat, severing everything right through to the bone of her spine, plunging her terrified soul into pitch darkness.

Bolt upright in bed, Siân clutched her head in her hands, expecting it to be lolling loose from her neck, a grisly hallowe'en pumpkin of bloody flesh. The shrill sound of screaming whirled around her room. She was alone, as always, in the early dawn of a Yorkshire summer, clutching her sweaty but otherwise unharmed head in the topmost bedroom of the White Horse and Griffin Hotel. Outside the attic window, the belligerent chorus of Whitby's seagull hordes shrieked on and on. To other residents of the hotel (judging by their rueful comments at the breakfast tables), these birds sounded like car alarms or circular saws or electric drills penetrating hardwood. Only to Siân, evidently, did they sound like her own death cries as she was being decapitated.

It was true that ever since the accident in Bosnia, Siân's dreams had treated her pretty roughly. For years on end she'd had her 'standard-issue' nightmare — the one in which she was chased through dark alleyways by a malevolent car. But at least in *that* dream she'd always wake up just before she fell beneath the wheels, whisked to the safety of the waking world, still flailing under the tangled sheets and blankets of her bed. Ever since she'd moved to Whitby, however, her dreams had lost what little good taste they'd once had, and now Siân was lucky if she got out of them alive.

The White Horse and Griffin had a plaque out front proudly declaring it had won *The Sunday Times* Golden Pillow Award, but Siân's pillow must be immune to the hotel's historically sedative charm. Tucked snugly under the ancient sloping roof of the

Mary Ann Hepworth room, with a velux window bringing her fresh air direct from the sea, Siân still managed to toss sleepless for hours before finally being lured into nightmare by the man with the giant hands. She rarely woke without having felt the cold steel of his blade carving her head off.

This dream of being first seduced, then murdered — always by a knife through the neck — had ensconced itself so promptly after her arrival in Whitby that Siân had asked the hotel proprietor if . . . if he happened to know how Mary Ann Hepworth had met her death. Already embarrassed that a science postgraduate like herself should stoop to such superstitious probings, she'd blushed crimson when he informed her that the room was named after a ship.

In the cold light of a Friday morning, swallowing hard through a throat she couldn't quite believe was still in one piece, Siân squinted at her watch. Ten to six. Two-and-a-bit hours to fill before she could start work. Two-and-a-bit hours before she could climb the one hundred and ninety-nine steps to the abbey churchyard and join the others at the dig.

A bath would pass the time, and would soak these faint mud-stains off her forearms, these barely perceptible discolorations ringing her flesh like alluvial deposits. But she was tired and irritable and there was a pain in her left hip — a nagging, bone-deep pain that had been getting worse and worse lately

3

— and she was in no mood to drag herself into the tub. What a lousy monk or nun she would have made, if she'd lived in medieval times. So reluctant to subject her body to harsh discipline, so lazy about leaving the warmth of her bed . . . ! So frightened of death.

This pain in her hip, and the hard lump that was manifesting in the flesh of her thigh just near where the pain was — it had to be bad news, very bad news. She should get it investigated. She wouldn't, though. She would ignore it, bear it, distract herself from it by concentrating on her work, and then one day, hopefully quite suddenly, it would be all over.

Thirty-four. She was, as of a few weeks ago, over half the age that good old Saint Hilda reached when she died. Seventh-century medical science wasn't quite up to diagnosing the cause, but Siân suspected it was cancer that had brought an end to Hilda's illustrious career as Whitby's founding abbess. Her photographic memory retrieved the words of Bede: 'It pleased the Author of our salvation to try her holy soul by a long sickness, in order that her strength might be made perfect in weakness.'

Made perfect in weakness! Was there a touch of bitter sarcasm in the Venerable Bede's account? No, almost certainly not. The humility, the serene stoicism of the medieval monastic mind — how terrifying it was, and yet how wonderful. If only *she* could think like that, feel like that, for just a few minutes!

All her fears, her miseries, her regrets, would be flushed out of her by the pure water of faith; she would see herself as a spirit distinct from her treacherous body, a bright feather on the breath of God.

All very well, but I'm still not having a bath, she thought grouchily.

Through the velux window she could see a trio of seagulls, hopping from roof-tile to roof-tile, chortling at her goose-pimpled, wingless body as she threw aside the bedclothes. She dressed hurriedly, got herself ready for the day. The best thing about hands-on archaeology like the Whitby dig was that no-one expected anybody to look glamorous, and you could wear the same old clothes day in, day out. She'd have to smarten herself up when she returned to her teaching rounds in the autumn; there was nothing like a lecture hall full of students, some of them young males, scrutinising you as if to say, 'Where did they dig *her* up?' to focus your mind on what skirt and top you ought to wear.

Before descending the stairs to the breakfast room, Siân took a swig from the peculiar little complimentary bottle of mineral water and looked out over the roof-tops of Whitby's east side. The rising sun glowed yellow and orange on the terracotta ridges. Obscured by the buildings and a litter of sails and boat-masts, the water of the river Esk twinkled indigo. Deep in Siân's abdomen, a twinge of pain made her wince. Was it indigestion, or something to do with the lump in her hip? She mustn't think about it. Go away, Venerable Bede! 'In the seventh year of her illness,' he wrote of Saint Hilda, 'the pain passed into her innermost parts.' Whereupon, of course, she died.

Siân went downstairs to the breakfast room, hoping that if she could find something to eat, the pain in her innermost parts might settle down. It was much too early, though, and the room was dim and deserted, with tea-towels shrouding the cereal boxes and the milk jug empty. Siân considered eating a banana, but it was the last one in the bowl and she felt, absurdly, that this would make the act sinful somehow. Instead she ate a couple of grapes and wandered around the room, touching each identically laid, melancholy table with her fingertips. She seated herself at one, thinking of the Benedictine monks and nuns in their refectories, forbidden to speak except for the reciting of Holy Scripture. Dreamily pretending she was one of them, she lifted her hands into the pale light and gestured in the air the mute signals for fish, for bread, for wine.

'Are you all right?'

Siân jerked, almost knocking a teacup off the table.

'Yes, yes,' she assured the Horse and Griffin's kitchen-maid, large as life in the doorway. 'Fine, thank you.' She sighed. 'Just going batty.'

'I don't wonder,' said the kitchen-maid. 'All them bodies.'

'Bodies?'

'The skeletons you've been diggin' up.' The girl made a face. 'Sixty of 'em, I read in the *Whitby Gazette*.'

'Sixty graves. We haven't actually—'

'D'you 'ave to touch 'em? I'd be sickened off. You wear gloves, I 'ope.'

Siân smiled, shook her head. The girl's look of horrified awe beamed at her across the breakfast room like a ray, and she basked shyly in it: Siân the dare-devil. For the sake of the truth, she ought to disabuse this girl of her fantasy of archaeologists rooting elbow-deep in grisly human remains, and tell her that the dig was really very like gardening except less eventful. But instead, she raised her hands and wiggled the fingers, as if to say, *Ordinary mortals cannot know what I have touched.*

'Braver than me, you are,' said the girl, unveiling the milk.

To help time pass, Siân crossed the bridge from the less corrupted east side to the more newfangled west, and strolled along Pier Road towards the sea. Thinly gilded with sunlight, the façades of the amusement arcades and clairvoyants' cabins looked almost grand, their windows and shuttered doors deflecting the glare. Siân dawdled in Marine Parade to peer through the window of what, until 1813, had been the Whitby Commercial Newsroom. 'The Award-Winning Dracula Experience' said the poster, followed by a list of attractions, including voluptuous female vampires and Christopher Lee's cape.

The fish quay, deserted just now, was nevertheless infested with loitering seagulls. They wandered around aimlessly in the sunrise, much as the town's young men would do after sunset, or simply snoozed on top of crates and the roofs of the moored boats.

Siân walked to the lighthouse, then left the terra firma of Aislaby sandstone to tread the timber deck of the pier's end. Careful not to snag the heels of her shoes on the gaps in the wood, she allowed herself the queasy thrill of peeking at the restless waves churning far beneath her feet. She wasn't sure if she could swim anymore; it had been a long time.

She stood at the very end of the west pier and cupped her hand across her brow to look over at the east one. The two piers were like outstretched arms curving into the ocean, to gather boats from the wild waters of the North Sea into the safety of Whitby harbour. Siân was standing on a giant fingertip.

She consulted her watch and walked back to the mainland. Her work was on the other side.

Ascending the East Cliff, half-way up the one hundred and ninety-nine stone steps, Siân paused for a breather. Much as she loved to walk, she'd overdone it, perhaps, so early in the day. She should keep in mind that instead of going to sit at a desk now, she was going to spend the whole day digging in the earth.

Siân traced the imperfections of the stone step with her shoe, demarcating the erosion caused by the foot traffic of centuries. On just this spot, this wide plateau-like step amongst many narrow ones, the townspeople of ancient Whitby laid down the coffins they must carry up to the churchyard, and had paused, black-clad and red-faced, before resuming their doleful ascent. Only now that tourists and archaeologists had finally taken the place of mourners did these steps no longer accommodate dead people — apart from the occasional obese American holiday-maker who collapsed with a heart attack before reaching the hallowed photo-opportunity.

Siân peered down towards Church Street and saw a man jogging — no, not jogging, running — towards the steps. At his side, a dog — a gorgeous animal, the size of a spaniel perhaps, but with a lovely thick coat, like a wolf's. The man wasn't bad-looking himself, broad-shouldered and well-muscled, pounding the cobbled surface of the street with his expensive-looking trainers. He was dressed in shorts and a loose, thin sweatshirt, a shivery proposition in the early morning chill, but he was obviously well up to it. His face was calm as he ran, his dark brown hair, free of sweat, flopping back and forth across his brow. The dog looked up at him frequently as he ran, revealing the vanilla and caramel colouring in its mane.

I want, I want, I want, thought Siân, then turned away, blushing. Thirty-four years old, and still thinking like a child! Saint Hilda would have been ashamed of her. And what exactly was she hankering after, anyway: the man or the dog? She wasn't even sure.

Another glance at her watch confirmed there was still a little while to fill before the first of her colleagues was likely to roll up. They all slept soundly, she gathered, in spite of the dawn chorus.

'Hello-o!'

She turned. The handsome young man was sprinting up the hundred and ninety-nine steps, as easily as if he were on flat ground. His dog was bounding ahead, narrowing the distance to Siân two steps at a time. For an instant Siân felt primeval fear at the approach of a powerful fanged creature, then relaxed as the dog scudded to a halt and sat to attention in front of her, panting politely, its head tilted to one side, just like a dog on a cheesy greeting card.

'He won't hurt you!' said the man, catching up, panting a little himself now.

'I can see that,' she said, hesitantly reaching forward to stroke the dog's mane.

'He's got an eye for the ladies,' said the man.

'Nothing personal, then.'

The man came to a halt one step below her, so as not to intimidate her with his tallness: he must be six foot three, at least. With every breath his pectorals swelled into his shirt in two faint haloes of sweat, and faded again.

'You're very fit,' she said, trying to keep her tone the same as if she were saying, 'You're out and about very early.'

'Well, if you don't use it,' he shrugged, 'you lose it.'

The dog was becoming quietly ecstatic, pushing his downy black brow up towards Siân's palm, following her fingers with his eyes, hoping she would get around to stroking the back of his head, the right ear, the left, the part of the right ear she'd missed the first time.

'What sort of dog is he?'

'Finnish Lapphund,' said the man, squatting on his haunches, as if seeking to qualify for a bit of stroking himself.

'Beautiful.'

'A hell of a lot of work.'

She knelt, carefully so that he wouldn't notice any problem with her left leg. 'Doesn't look it,' she said, stroking the dog's back all the way to his plushly fringed tail. All three of them were eye to eye now.

'You bring out his contemplative side, obviously,'

the man remarked, grinning. 'With me, it's a different story. I'll be an Olympic runner by the time he's through with me.'

Siân stroked on and on, a little self-conscious about the ardour with which she was combing the creature's sumptuous pelt. 'You must have known what you were taking on when you got him,' she suggested.

'Well, no, he was actually my father's dog. My father died three weeks ago.'

Siân stopped stroking. 'Oh, I'm sorry.'

'No need. He and I weren't close.' The dog, bereft of caresses, was poking his snout in the air, begging for more. The man obliged, ruffling the animal's ears, pulling the furry face towards his. 'I didn't like our dad much, did I, hmm? Grumpy old man, wasn't 'e?'

Siân noticed the size of the man's hands: unusually large. A superstitious chill tickled her spine, like a tiny trickle of water. She distracted herself from it by noting the estuary twang of the man's accent.

'Did you come up from London?'

'Yeah.' He frowned a little, intent on proving he could please the dog as much as the next pair of hands. 'To bury the old man. And to sort out the house. Haven't decided what I'll do yet. It's in Loggerhead's Yard, so it's worth a mint. I might sell it; I might live in it. As a building, it's a hell of a lot nicer than my flat in West Kilburn.' He cast a deprecating glance back at the town, as if to add, *Except of course it's in bloody Whitby*.

'Did you live here as a kid?'

'Many, many, long, long years,' he affirmed, in a querulous tone of weary melodrama. 'Couldn't get out fast enough.'

Siân puzzled over the two halves of his statement, and couldn't help thinking there was a flaw in his logic somewhere.

'I like this place myself,' she said. It surprised her to hear herself saying it — given the nightmares and the insomnia, she had good reason to associate Whitby with misery. But it was true: she liked the place.

'But you're not *from* here, are you?'

'No. I'm an archaeologist, working at the dig.'

'Cool! The sixty skeletons, right?'

'Among other things, yes.' She looked away from him, to register her disapproval of his sensationalist instincts, but if he noticed, he didn't give a toss.

'Wow,' he said. 'Gothic.'

'Anglian, actually, as far as we can tell.'

Her attempt to put him in his place hung in the air between them, sounding more and more snooty as she replayed it in her head. She returned her attention to the dog, trying to salvage things by stroking the parts the man wasn't stroking.

'What's his name?'

He hesitated for a moment. 'Hadrian.'

She snorted helplessly. 'That's . . . that's an exceptionally crap name. For *any* dog, but especially this one.'

'Isn't it!' he beamed. 'My dad was a Roman history buff, you see.'

'And *your* name?'

Again he hesitated. 'Call me Mack.'

'Short for something?'

'Magnus.' His pale blue eyes narrowed. 'Latin for "great". Grisly, isn't it?'

'Grisly?'

'Sounds like I've got a big head or something.'

'I'll reserve judgement on that. It's a fine, ancient name, anyway.'

'You *would* say that, wouldn't you?'

The familiarity of his tone worried her a bit. What delicate work it was, this business of conversing with strangers of the other sex! No wonder she hardly ever attempted it anymore . . .

'What do you mean?' she said.

'You know, being an archaeologist and all that.'

'I'm not actually a fully-fledged archaeologist. Still studying.'

'Oh? I would've thought . . .' He caught himself before he could say 'at your age' or anything like that, but the implication stabbed straight into Siân —

straight into her innermost parts, so to speak. Yes, damn it, she didn't look like a peachy young thing anymore. What she'd gone through in Bosnia — and since — was written and underlined on her face. "It pleased the Author of our salvation ..." Pleased Him to put her body and soul through Hell. In order that her strength might be made perfect in weakness. In order that people she'd only just met would think she was awfully old to be studying for a degree.

'I would've thought archaeology was a hands-on kind of thing,' he said.

'So it is. I'm a qualified conservator, actually, specialising in the preservation of paper and parchment. I just fancied a change, thought I should get out more. There's a nice mixture of people at this dig. Some have been archaeologists for a million years. Some are just kids, getting their first pay-packet.'

'And then there's you.'

'Yes, then there's me.'

He was staring at her; in fact, both he and his dog were staring at her, and in much the same way, too: eyes wide and sincere, waiting for her to give them the next piece of her.

'I'm Siân,' she said, at last.

'Lovely name. Meaning?'

'Sorry?'

'Siân. In Welsh, it means ... ?'

She racked her brains for the derivation of her name. 'I don't think it means anything much. Jane, I suppose. Just plain Jane.'

'You're not plain,' he spoke up immediately, grateful for the chance to make amends.

To hide her embarrassment, she heaved herself to her feet. 'Well, it's nearly time I started work.' And she steeled herself for the remaining hundred steps.

'Can I walk with you as far as the church? There's a run I can do with Hadrian near there, back down to the town . . .'

'Sure,' she said lightly. He mustn't see her limping. She would do what she could to prevent his attention straying below her waist.

'So . . .' she said, as they set off together, the dog scampering ahead, then scooting back to circle them. 'Now that your father's funeral's over, do you have much more sorting out to do?'

'It's finished, really. But I've got a research paper to write, for my final year of Medicine. So, I'm using Dad's house as a kind of . . . solitary confinement. To get on with it, you know. There's a lot of distractions in London. Even worse distractions than *this* fellow . . .' And he aimed a slow, playful kick at Hadrian.

'You're partaking of a fine Whitby tradition, then,' said Siân. 'Think of those monks and nuns sitting in their bare cells, reading and scribing all day.'

He laughed. 'Oh, I'm sure they got up to a hell of a lot more than that.'

Was this bawdy crack, and the wink that accompanied it, supposed to have any relevance to the two of them, or was it just the usual cynicism that most people had about monastic life? Probably just the usual cynicism, because when they ascended to the point where the turrets of Whitby Abbey were visible, he said: 'Ah! The lucrative ruins!' He flung his right arm forward, unfurling his massive hand in a grandiose gesture. 'See Whitby Abbey and die!'

Siân felt her hackles rise, yet at the same time she was tickled by his theatricality. She'd always detested shy, cringing men.

'If the Abbey'd had a bit more money over the centuries,' she retorted, 'it wouldn't *be* ruins.'

'Oh come on,' he teased. 'Ruins are where the real money is, surely? People love it.' He mimicked an American sightseer posing for his camera-toting wife: '"Take a pitcha now, Wilma, of me wid dese here ruins of antiquiddy behind me!"'

Squinting myopically, acting the buffoon, he ought to have looked foolish, but his clowning only served to accentuate how handsome he was. His irreverent grin, and the way he inhabited his body with more grace than his gangly frame ought to allow, were an attractive combination for Siân — a combination she'd been attracted to before, almost fatally. She'd have to be careful with this young man, that's for sure, if she didn't want a re-run of . . . of the Patrick fiasco.

'Antiquity *is* exciting,' she said. 'It's *good* that people are willing to come a long way to see it. They walk up these stone stairs towards that abbey, and they feel they're literally following in the footsteps of medieval monks and ancient kings. They see those turrets poking up over the headland, and it takes them back eight hundred years . . .'

'Ah, but that thing up there isn't the real Whitby Abbey, is it? It's a reconstruction: some tourist body's idea of what a medieval abbey should look like.'

'That's not true.'

'Didn't it all fall down ages ago, and they built it up in completely the wrong shape?'

'No, that's not true,' she insisted, feeling herself tempted to argue heatedly with a complete stranger — something she hadn't done since Patrick. She ought to dismiss his ignorance with the lofty condescension it deserved, but instead she said, 'Come up and I'll show you.'

'What?' he said, but she was already quickening her pace. 'Wait!'

She stumped ahead, leading him past Saint Mary's churchyard, past the cliffside trail to Caedmon's Trod — the alternative path back to the town below, along which he'd meant to run with Hadrian. Teeth clenched with effort, she stumped up another flight of steps leading to the abbey.

'It's all right, I believe you!' Magnus protested as he dawdled in her wake, hoping she'd come round, but she led him straight on to the admission gate. He baulked at the doorway, only to see his cheerfully disloyal dog trotting across the threshold.

'Bastard,' he muttered as he followed.

Inside, there was a sign warning visitors that all pets must be on a leash, and there was a man at the admissions counter waiting to be handed £1.70. Siân, so used to wandering freely in and out of the abbey grounds that she'd forgotten there was a charge for non-archaeologists, paused to take stock. Mack's running shorts, whatever else they might contain, clearly had no provision for a wallet.

'He's with me,' she declared, and led the hapless Magnus past the snack foods and pamphlets, through the portal to antiquity. It all happened so fast, Hadrian was dashing across the turf, already half-way to the 12th century, before the English Heritage man could say a word.

Siân stood in the grassy emptiness of what had once been the abbey's nave. The wind flapped at her skirt. She pointed up at the towering stone arches, stark and skeletal against the sky. The thought of anyone — well, specifically this man at her side — being immune to the primitive grandeur and the tragic devastation of this place, provoked her to a righteous lecture.

'Those three arches there,' she said, making sure he was looking where her finger pointed (he was — and so was his dog), 'those arches are originally from the south wall, yes, and when they were reconstructed in the 1920s, they were propped up against the northern boundary wall, yes. Rather odd, I admit. But it's all the original masonry, you know. And at least those arches are safe now. We'd love to restore them to their original position, but they're better off where they are than in a pile of rubble — or don't you think so?'

'I'm sorry, I'm sorry!' he pleaded facetiously. 'I didn't know I was treading on your toes ...'

'I have some books and brochures that explain everything, the whole history,' she said. 'You can read those — I'll give them to you. A nice parcel. Loggerhead's Yard, wasn't it?'

'Oh, but no, really,' he grimaced, flushing with embarrassment. 'I should buy them myself.'

'Nonsense. You're welcome to them.'

'But ... but they're *yours*. You've spent money ...'

'Nonsense, I've got what I needed from them; they're not doing me any good now.' Seeing him squirm, she was secretly enjoying her modest subversion of 21st-century capitalism, her feeble imitation of the noble Benedictine principle of common ownership. 'Besides, I can smell cynicism on you, Mr Magnus. I'd like to get rid of that, if I can.'

He laughed uneasily, and lifted one elbow to call attention to his sweat-soaked armpits.

'Are you sure it's not the smell of B.O.?'

'Quite sure,' she said, noting that two of her colleagues were, at last, straggling into view. 'Now, I think it's about time I started work. It was lovely to meet you. And Hadrian, of course.'

She shook his hand, and allowed herself one more ruffle of the dog's mane. Nonplussed, Magnus backed away.

A few seconds later, when she was already far away from him, he called after her:

'Happy digging!'

That night, Siân fell asleep with unusual ease. Instead of spending hours looking at the cast-iron fireplace and the wooden clothes rack growing gradually more distinct in the moonlight, she slept in profound darkness.

I'm sleeping, she thought as she slept. *How divine.*

'Oh, flesh of my flesh,' whispered a voice in her ear. 'Forgive me . . .' And the cold, slightly serrated edge of a large knife pressed into her windpipe. With a yelp, she leapt into wakefulness, but not before the flesh of her throat had yawned open and released a welter of blood.

Upright in bed, she clutched her neck, to keep her life clamped safely inside. The skin was unbroken, a little damp with perspiration. She let go, groaning irritably.

It wasn't even morning: it was pitch-dark, and the seagulls were silent — still fast asleep, wherever it is that seagulls sleep. Siân peered at her watch, but it was the old-fashioned kind (she didn't like digital watches) and she couldn't see a thing.

Ten minutes later she was dressed and ready for going out. Packed in a shoulder bag were the books and pamphlets for Magnus: 'Saint Hilda and her Abbey at Whitby', *A History of Whitby*, the Pitkin guide to 'Life in a Monastery', and several others. She slung the bag behind her hip and shrugged experimentally to confirm it stayed put; she didn't want it swinging forward and tripping her up. Getting your neck slashed in a dream was one thing; *breaking* your neck while trying to get down a steep flight of stairs in the dead of night was quite another.

In the event, she managed without any problem, and was soon standing in the cold breeze of the White Horse and Griffin's side lane, cobbles underfoot. The town was so quiet she could hear her own breathing, and Church Street was closed to traffic in any case, yet still she ventured forward from the alley very, very carefully — a legacy of her accident in Bosnia. Even in a pedestrianised cul-de-sac in a small Yorkshire town at four in the morning, you never knew what might come ripping around the corner.

In the dark, Whitby looked strange to Siân — neither modern nor medieval, which were the only two ways she was accustomed to perceiving it. In the daylight hours, she was either working in the shadow of the abbey ruins, coaxing the remains of stunted Northumbrians out of the antique clay, or she was weaving through crowds of shoppers and tourists, that vulgar throng of pilgrims with mobile phones clutched to their cheeks or pop groups advertised on their chests. Now, in the unpeopled stillness of night, Whitby looked, to Siân, distinctly Victorian. She didn't know why — the buildings and streets were much older than that, mostly. But it wasn't a matter of architecture; it was a matter of atmosphere. The glow of the streetlamps could almost be gaslight; the obscure buildings and darkened doorways scowled with menace, like a movie backdrop for yet another version of Bram Stoker's *Dracula*. Any alleyway, it seemed to Siân, could disgorge at any moment the caped figure of the Count, or a somnambulistic young woman of unnatural pallor, her white night-gown stained with blood.

Gothic. That's what the word 'Gothic' meant to most people nowadays. Nothing to do with the original Germanic tribe, or even the pre-Renaissance architectural style. The realities of history had been swept aside by Hollywood vampires and narcissistic rock singers with too much mascara on. And here she was, as big a sucker as anyone: walking down Church Street at four in the morning, imagining the whole town to be crawling with Victorianesque undead. Even the Funtasia joke shop, which during the day sold plastic vampire fangs and whoopee cushions, seemed at this godforsaken hour to be a genuinely creepy establishment, the sort of place inside which rats and madmen might be lurking.

The house in Loggerhead's Yard was easy to find; when she'd asked about it in the hotel, half a dozen people jostled to give her directions. Magnus's father had been well known in the town and all the locals took a keen interest whenever a death freed up a hunk of prime real estate. Only when Siân approached the front door did she have her first doubts about what she'd come here to do. An action which, in daylight with people strolling round about, would look like a casual errand, seemed anything but casual now — the eerie stillness and the ill-lit, empty streets made her feel as if she were up to no good. She could be a thief, a cat burglar, a rapist, tiptoeing so as not to wake the virtuously sleeping world, squinting at a slit in a stranger's door, preparing to slide a foreign object through it. What if the door should open suddenly, to reveal Magnus, still naked and warm from his bed, rubbing his eyes? Or what about the dog? Surely he would go berserk at the sound of her fumblings at the mail slot! Siân steeled her nerves for an explosion of barking as she fed the books and pamphlets, one by one, through the dark vent, but they dropped softly onto the floor within, and that was all. Hadrian was either uninspired by the challenges of being a guard dog, or asleep. Asleep on the bed of his master, perhaps. Two muscular males nestled side by side, different species but both devilishly handsome.

For goodness' sake, she sighed to herself, turning away. *When will you grow up?*

Bag empty and weightless on her shoulder, she hurried back to the hotel.

Siân had never been fond of weekends. They were all very well for people with hobbies or a frustrated desire to luxuriate in bed, but she would rather be working. Half the reason she'd switched from paper conservation to archaeology was that it required her to show up, no matter what, at the appointed hour, and dig. It wasn't easy, especially in raw weather, but it was better than wasting the whole day thinking about the past — her own past, that is.

Saint Benedict had the right idea: a community of monastics keeping to a strict ritual seven days a week, helping each other get out of bed with (as he put it) 'gentle encouragement, on account of the excuses to which the sleepy are addicted'. Siân knew all about those.

To prevent herself moping, she spent most of her weekends wandering around Whitby, back and forth across the swing bridge, from pier to pier, from cliff to cliff. She'd walk until she tired herself out, and then lie on her bed in the Mary Ann Hepworth room with a book on her lap, watching the roof-tops change colour, until it was time for her to go to sleep and get what was coming to her.

This week, Saturday passed more quickly than usual. Her early-morning excursion to the house in Loggerhead's Yard had been quite thrilling in its stealthy way, and afterwards she fell into a long, mercifully dreamless doze. She woke quite rested, with only three-quarters of the weekend left to endure.

In the afternoon, while she had a bite of lunch at the Whitby Mission and Seafarer's Centre, a gusty breeze flapped the yellowing squares of paper pinned to the notice-board near the door. *'Don't leave Fido out in the cold,'* said one fluttering page. *'We have a separate coffee lounge where pets are always welcome.'* Siân left the ruins of her jacket potato consolidating on her plate and walked over to the opposite lounge to have a peek inside. Her nose nudged through a veil of cigarette smoke. Strange dogs with strange owners looked up at the newcomer.

On her way out of the Mission, Siân paused at the book-case offering books for 50p each, and rummaged through the thrillers, romances and anthologies of local writers' circles. There was a cheap, mass-produced New Testament there, too. What a come-down since the days when a Bible was a unique and priceless object, inscribed on vellum from an entire flock of sheep! Siân closed her eyes, imagined a cloister honeycombed in sunlight, with a long rank of desks and tonsured heads, perfect silence except for the faint scratching of pen-nibs.

'Now *here's* a blast from the past!' brayed the disc jockey on the radio. 'Hands up anyone who bopped along to Culture Club when they had this hit — come on, 'fess up!'

Siân fled.

Early on Sunday morning, not long after getting her throat slit, Siân was out and about again, her hastily-washed hair steaming. She couldn't be bothered blow-drying it, and besides, *now* was when she ought to be going — at exactly the same time as she'd set off for work on Friday. If Magnus and Hadrian were creatures of habit, this would send them running after her any minute now.

She walked along Church Street, quite slowly, from the hotel façade to the foot of the hundred and ninety-nine steps and back again — twice — but no chance meeting occurred.

Tantalised by the thought of the man and his dog running high up on the East Cliff, in the wild grasses flanking the abbey ramparts, she climbed Caedmon's Trod until she could see the Donkey Field. No chance meeting occurred here, either, at least not with Magnus and Hadrian. Instead, she met a bored-looking boy and his somewhat frazzled dad, returning from what had clearly been a less than inspirational visit to the abbey.

'Another really interesting thing that monasteries used to do,' the father was saying, in a pathetic, last-ditch attempt to get the child excited, 'was give sanctuary to murderers.'

Siân saw a flicker of interest in the kid's eyes as she squeezed past him on the narrow monks' trod.

'Has Whitby got McDonalds,' he asked his dad, 'or only fish and chips?'

It was Monday afternoon before Siân saw Magnus again. In the morning, she loitered around the town centre before work, in an irritable, shaky state. Her nightmare hadn't yet receded, and her throat was sore where, in a befuddled attempt to deflect the knife, she had hit herself with her own hand. The lump in her thigh throbbed like hell.

In the town's deserted market square, on a bench, someone had discarded a copy of the current *Whitby Gazette*. With half an hour still to kill before 8 a.m., Siân settled down to read it. For some reason though, every single article in the *Gazette* struck her as

28

monumentally depressing. Not just the sad stories, like the one about the much-loved local janitor dying of cancer ('He never moaned about his illness and was always cheerful', according to a colleague — a chip off Saint Hilda's block, then). No, even the stories about a holidaymaker being struck by lightning and surviving, or a charity snail-eating contest, or the long-overdue restoration of Egton Bridge, brought Siân closer and closer to irrational tears. She flipped the pages faster, through the property section, until she was on the back page, staring at an advertisement for a beauty clinic on the West Cliff. 'Sun-dome with facial and leg boosters' it said, and to Siân this seemed like the most heartbreakingly sad phrase she'd ever read this side of the Book of Ecclesiastes.

Get a grip, she counselled herself, and laid the paper aside. She noticed that someone had joined her on the bench: an obese, spiky-haired punkette, an unusual sight in Whitby — almost as unusual as a monk. Siân goggled just a few seconds too long at the infestation of silver piercings on the girl's brow, nose and ears, and was given a warning scowl in return. Chastened, she looked down. At the punkette's feet sat a dog, to help the girl beg perhaps. Apart from the pictogram for 'anarchy' doodled on his wheat-coloured flank in black felt-tip, he was a very ordinary-looking dog, a Labrador maybe — nowhere near as beautiful as Hadrian.

Face it: compared to Hadrian, every other dog was plain.

At ten to eight, Siân began to climb the hundred and ninety-nine steps and, gazing for a moment across the harbour, she suddenly spotted Hadrian and Magnus on the other side, two tiny figures sprinting along Marine Parade. Her melancholy turned at once to a sort of indignant excitement. Why would they choose *there* to run instead of here on *her* side? They must be avoiding her! Surely nobody could prefer the stink of raw fish and the pierside's dismal panorama of amusement parlours and pubs to what lay at the foot of the church steps ...

Her sudden, fervid impulse to jump up and down and wave to Mack, despite the fact that there was no chance of him noticing, alarmed her — clearly, she was farther gone than she'd thought, and should make an immediate start on restoring her sanity before it was too late.

I am here, she reminded herself, *to work. I am not here to be torn apart. I am not here to be treated like dirt.*

She imagined her emotions embodied in the form of a hysterical novice nun, and her judgement as the wise and kindly abbess, counselling restraint. She visualised the bare interior of one of Saint Hilda's prayer-cells lit up gold and amber with sunbeams, a merciful ebbing away of confusion, a soul at peace.

*   *   *

When Siân reached the burial site, Pru was already lifting off the blue tarpaulins, exposing the damp soil. Towards the edges of the excavation, the clay was somewhat soggier than it needed to be, having absorbed some rainfall over the weekend in addition to its ritual hosing last thing Friday afternoon. Siân was glad her appointed rectangle was towards the middle of the quarter acre. All right, maybe Saint Hilda wouldn't have approved of her desire to keep her knees dry at the expense of her fellow toilers, but the sheath of Tubigrip under her tights lost some of its elastic every time she washed it, so she'd rather it stayed clean, thank you very much.

'Sleep well?' asked Pru, rolling up another tarpaulin, exposing Siân's own appointed shallow grave.

'No, not really,' said Siân.

'Lemme guess — you stayed up to watch that movie about the robbery that goes wrong. The one with . . . oh, what's-her-name?' Regurgitation of facts was not Pru's *forte*. 'The one who's gained so much weight recently.'

'I'm sorry, I haven't a clue,' said Siân.

Jeff was next to arrive, a wizened old hippy who seemed to have been on every significant dig in Britain since the war. Then Keira and Trevor, a husband-and-wife team who were due to lay down their trowels and mattocks tomorrow and flee to the warmer and better-paid climes of a National Geographic dig in the Middle East. Who would replace them? Very nice people, according to Nina, the supervisor. Coming all the way from north Wales.

By ten past, everyone was on site and working, distributed like medieval potato harvesters over the sub-divided ground. Fourteen living bodies, scratching in the ground for the subtle remains of dead ones, peering at gradations in soil colour that could signal the vanished presence of a coffin or a pelvis, winkling pale fragments into the light which could, please God, be teeth.

The skeletons exhumed so far had all been buried facing east, the direction of Jerusalem, to help Judgement Day run more smoothly. Four years from now, when the research would be completed and the bones re-buried with the aid of a JCB and vicar to bless them, they'd have to sort out their direction for themselves.

Today, one of the girls was in a bad mood, her mouth clownishly downturned, her eyes avoiding contact with the young man working next to her. Yesterday, they'd been exchanging secret smiles, winks, *sotto voce* consultations. Today, they did their best to pretend they weren't kneeling side by side; separated by mere inches, they cast expectant glances not at each other but at Nina, as if hoping she might assign them to different plots farther apart. A cautionary spectacle, thought Siân. A living parable (as Saint Hilda might call it) of the fickleness of human love.

'I think I may've found something,' said someone several hours later, holding up an encrusted talon which might, once it was X-rayed, prove to be a coffin pin.

At four-thirty, as Siân was walking past Saint Mary's churchyard on her way down to the hundred and ninety-nine steps, she spotted Hadrian's head poking up over the topmost one.

'Hush!' he barked in greeting. 'Hush, hush!'

Siân hesitated, then waved. Magnus was nowhere to be seen.

Hadrian ran towards her, pausing only to scale the church's stone boundary and sniff the base of Caedmon's Cross. Deciding not to piss on England's premier Anglo-Saxon poet, he bounded back onto the path and had an exuberant reunion with Siân.

By the time Magnus joined them, she was on one knee, her hands buried deep in the dog's mane, and Hadrian was jumping up and down to lick her face.

'Excuse me, I'm just going overboard here,' she said, too delighted with the dog's affection to care what a fool she must look.

Mack wasn't wearing his running gear this afternoon; instead, his powerful frame was disguised in a button-down shirt, Chinos and some sort of expensive suede-y jacket. He was carrying a large plastic bag, but apart from that he looked like a young doctor who'd answered his beeper at a London brasserie and been persuaded to make a house call. Siân had trouble accepting he could look like this; she'd imagined him (she realised now) permanently dressed in shorts and T-shirt, running around Whitby in endless circles. She laughed at the thought, her inhibitions loosened by the excesses she was indulging with Hadrian. Casting her eyes down in an effort to reassure Mack that she wasn't laughing at him, she caught sight of his black leather shoes, huge things too polished to be true. She giggled even more. Her own steel-capped boots were slathered in mud, and her long bedraggled skirt was filthy at the knees.

'You and Hadrian better not get too friendly,' Mack remarked. 'He might run off with one of your precious old bones.'

It was such a feeble joke that Siân didn't think anyone could possibly blame her for ignoring it. She heaved herself to her feet and, fancying she could feel his eyes on her dowdiness, she sobered up in a hurry.

'Have you read any of the books and pamphlets?' she said.

He snorted. 'You sound like a Jehovah's Witness, on a follow-up visit.'

'Never mind that. Have you read them?' *Be firm with him*, she was thinking.

'Of course,' he smiled.

'And?'

'Very interesting,' he said, watching her straighten her shapeless cagoule. 'More interesting than my research, anyway.'

As they fell into step with each other towards the town, Siân rifled her memory for the subject of his paper. It took her a good fifteen seconds to realise she'd never actually asked him about it.

They'd reached the bench on the resting-place near the top of the hundred and ninety-nine steps, and he indicated with a wave of his hand that they should sit down. This they did, with Hadrian settled against Siân's skirt, and Mack carefully lowering the plastic bag onto the ground between his lustrous shoes. Judging by the sharp corners bulging through the plastic, it contained a large cardboard box.

'That's not your research paper in there, is it?' she asked.

'No,' he said.

'What is it?'

'A surprise.'

Michael, one of Siân's colleagues from the dig, walked past the bench where they were sitting. He nodded in greeting as he descended the steps, looking slightly sheepish, unsure whether to introduce himself to Siân's new friend or pretend he hadn't trespassed on their privacy. It was a gauche little encounter, lasting no more than a couple of seconds, but Siân was ashamed to note that it gave her a secret thrill; how sweet it was to be mistaken for a woman sharing intimacy with a man! Let the whole world pass by this bench, in an orderly procession, to witness proof incarnate that she wasn't lonely!

For God's sake, get a grip! she reproached herself.

'My research,' said Mack, smirking a little, 'examines whether psittacosis is transferable from human to human.' His smirk widened into a full grin as she stared back at him with a blank expression. Siân wondered if he'd make her ask, but, commendably, he didn't. 'Psittacosis,' he explained, 'is what's popularly called parrot fever – if popular is the right word for a rare disease. It's a virus, and you catch it by inhaling the powdered . . . uh . . . faeces of caged birds. In humans, it manifests as a kind of pneumonia that's highly resistant to antibiotics. It used to be fatal, once upon a time.'

Siân wondered just how long ago, in his view, 'once upon a time' was. *She*, after all, had had to convince herself, after reading the 'Health & Safety' documents covering archaeological digs, that she wasn't frightened of catching anthrax or the Black Death.

'And this disease of yours,' she said. '*Is* it transferable from human to human?'

'The answer used to be "Maybe". I'm aiming to change that to a definite "No".'

'Hmm,' said Siân. Now that she'd been sitting for a minute, she was suddenly rather weary, and her left leg ached and felt swollen. 'Well, I'm sure that'll put some people's minds at rest.' It sounded condescending, and she had the uneasy feeling she was being a bitch. 'No, really. With diseases, it's always better to know, isn't it?' An inane comment, which reminded her of the lump in her thigh she was so determined to ignore. Irritably, she wiped her face. 'Sorry, I'm tired.'

'Another long day exhuming the dead?'

'No, I just didn't sleep so well last night.'

Again to his credit, he didn't pry. Instead he asked, 'Where do you keep them all, anyway? All the skeletons, I mean. Sixty of them, I read somewhere.' He nodded towards the East Cliff car park. 'Enough to fill a tourist bus.'

Siân giggled, picturing a large party of skeletons driving away, taking their last glimpse of Whitby through steamy coach windows as they began their long trip home.

'We've only found a few complete skeletons,' she said. 'Usually we find half-skeletons, or bits and pieces. Clay isn't as kind to bones as people imagine; in fact, they'd last longer just about anywhere else. Stuck in the ground, they crumble, they soften, they dissolve. Sometimes we'll find just a discoloration in the clay. A tell-tale shadow. That's why we have to be so careful, and so slow.'

'And these people you've dug up — who were they?'

A single word, Angles, sprang to Siân's mind, which made her feel a pang of guilty sorrow. How ruthless History was, taking as raw material the fiercely independent lives of sixty human individuals — sixty souls who, in life, fought for their right to be appreciated as unique, to earn the pride of their parents, the gratitude of their children, the loyalty of their colleagues — blending them all into the dirt, reducing them to a single archaic word.

'They were . . . Angles, probably,' she sighed. 'Difficult to be sure, until we do Carbon-14 dating on them. They lived after the Romans, anyway, and before the Norman Conquest.'

'Any treasures?'

'Treasures?'

'Gold, precious jewels . . . Bracelets and swords that can be buffed up to a sheen for the English Heritage brochures . . .'

Siân was determined not to be goaded by his tone. *Be firm with him*, she counselled herself. *Firm but dignified.*

'These people were early Christians,' she reminded him. 'They didn't believe in taking anything with them when they died. You know: "Naked came I into the world, and naked—"'

'Ha!' he scoffed, hoisting up a stiff index finger in a theatrical gesture of triumph. 'I've read up on this stuff now, don't forget! What about all those fancy trinkets they dug up in the 1920s, eh? Brooches, rings and whatever? Saint Hilda's nuns were rolling in it, weren't they?'

Siân leaned down, scorning to look at him, but instead stroking Hadrian tenderly. She spoke directly into the dog's furry, trusting face, as if she'd decided there was a great deal more point talking to Hadrian than to his master. 'People nowadays would *love* to believe the nuns were as corrupt as Hell,' she murmured. 'Did you know that, Hadrian?' She ruffled his ears, and nodded emphatically as though the shameless cynicism of humans was likely to beggar the belief of an innocent canine. 'It makes people feel smug, you see. Gives them a warm glow, to think of those religious idealists betraying their vows of poverty and swanning around in fancy gowns and jewellery.'

'And didn't they?'

Siân turned her attention to Magnus, looking him straight in the eyes while her hands carried on stroking. 'I prefer to give them the benefit of the doubt. Abbeys weren't just for monastic orders, you know; they were places of prayer and seclusion for ... well, anybody really. All sorts of rich people ended up in them — unmarried princesses, widowed queens ...

They'd retire there, servants and all. I like to think it's those powerful ladies that left behind the rings and brooches and buckles and whatnot.'

'You'd like to think,' he teased.

'Yes, I'd *like* to think,' she said, barely able to keep a sharp hiss of annoyance out of her voice. 'If there's no way of proving anything, why be cynical? Why not choose to think the best of people?'

His eyes twinkled with mischief.

'That's what I'm trying to do!' he protested mock-innocently. 'These old nuns sound as if they had a pretty dismal time. I want to cheer 'em up with a bit of the good life.'

Siân was imagining the 12th-century ruins she knew so well, trying to reconstruct, in her mind, the lost 7th-century original that the Vikings had destroyed.

'Funny what "the good life" means now . . .' she said wistfully. 'And what it used to mean . . .'

'Back in the Middle Ages when *you* were a nun?' he ribbed her. Then, sensing he'd gone too far, he hoisted up his plastic bag and carefully removed the cardboard box from it.

'Anyway, I want to show you something. Something I'm sure you'll appreciate more than anyone else, being a — what was it again? — a conserva-tionist?'

'Conservator,' she said, intrigued despite herself

as Mack opened the box to reveal, in a nest of crumpled toilet paper, a glass liquor bottle without any label, discoloured and dull, clearly antique. Inside the bottle was a large candle – no, not a candle, a tight scroll of papers. Water damage, evidently followed by ill-managed drying, had fused the layers of the scroll together into a puckered cylinder. There was handwritten text on the outermost layer, and the few capital letters Siân could make out at a glance were unmistakably 19th- or even 18th-century.

I want, I want, I want, she thought.

Mack held the bottle up close to her face, turning it slowly so the scroll revealed its text like the beginning of a web-page stored in the world's most ancient VDU.

'Look,' he said. 'You can still read it.'

Confession of Thos. Peirson, in the Year of Our Lord 1788
In the full and certain Knowledge that my Time is nigh,
for my good Wife has even now

That was as much of the text as was visible before it swallowed itself inside the roll.

'Where did you find this?' Too late, she heard the tremor of excitement in her voice, and – damn! – he noticed too, and grinned.

'I didn't find it, my dad did. It turned up in the foundations of Tin Ghaut when the town planners demolished it in 1959. He took it home before the bulldozers came back.'

Siân watched him replace the bottle in its nest of toilet paper. She took a breath, priming her voice for what she hoped would be a casual, matter-of-fact tone.

'That scroll — it could be unrolled, you know. We could find out what this man was confessing.'

'I don't think so,' said Mack, fingering the glass regretfully. 'I've tried to get the papers out. With forceps, even. But the paper's gone rigid, and it's wider than the neck of the bottle. Of course I could just break it open, but the thing is, the glass never got broken all this time, even when it was dug up by bloody great earthmovers. My dad thought that was a miracle, and it *is* kind of cool, I must admit. Smashing it now would be . . . I don't know . . . wrong somehow.'

Siân was touched by this glimmer of rudimentary morality when it came to preserving ancient things, but also impatient with his ignorance.

'We have tools to slice the bottle open without smashing it,' she said. 'We could open the bottle, extract the papers, gently separate them, read them...'

'Who's "we"?' he challenged her gently. 'You and me?'

Siân smiled, keen to stay on the right side of him. The thought of him closing the lid on his treasure box and carrying that scroll out of her life was hard to bear. *Give it to me, give it to me, give it to me*, she was thinking.

'There's a man I know at the University of Northumbria who could do the bottle for me,' she said. 'The papers I could do myself, right here.'

'Mm.' He sounded non-committal. Hadrian had wandered off, restless, miffed that the humans had allowed both the stroking and the running to lapse. He was in Saint Mary's churchyard again, pondering the bas-relief horses stabled at the base of Caedmon's Cross — horses that looked puzzlingly like toy dogs in a kennel.

'So . . .' said Siân. 'What do you think? May I?'

Mack reached into the box, and lifted the prize back into view.

'Are you sure you can put it all back together? Just the way it is now?' He handled the bottle firmly but with great tenderness. *You'll make a good doctor*, Siân thought.

'Sure,' she replied. 'A thin seam in the glass, that's all you'll see. And we'll do it where hardly anyone would think of looking.'

He raised one eyebrow dubiously. 'We will, will we?'

But, God bless him, he handed it over. One moment it was in his hands, the next she had received it into hers. Flesh brushed against flesh during the transfer.

'Trust me,' she said, as a thrill passed through her from wrist to toe, like a benign electric current looking for earth.

It was very late that night before she could begin. Neville, her pal at the University of Northumbria who could cut the bottle open, was unavailable to see her until he'd finished giving his evening lectures, and then he had some story about his wife expecting him at home. Siân forced him to call his wife on his mobile and tell her he had a quick job to do. Then she flattered him about his way with a laser.

'Honestly, Siân, can't it wait till tomorrow?' Neville had complained as he led her into his sanctum, switching on lights he'd only recently turned off.

'This thing has been waiting for me since 1788,' she replied.

Hours later, in the privacy of the Mary Hepworth Room, Siân fondled the paper scroll with gloved fingers. It was light, as she'd expected from its loss of moisture, but also much more brittle than she'd hoped. Any fantasies she might have entertained of simply unrolling the sheets and smoothing them out flat were out of the question. Progress would be slow, methodical, painstaking — as always when rescuing any-thing from the ravages of time. Nothing ever came easy.

This paper had clearly been sized with a lot of gelatine — and a rich gelatine at that, involving generous amounts of animal skin, hooves, bones. A nice smooth glossy paper it must have been, in its day — but water damage had turned the gelatine to glue. And whatever had dried the soggy paper out again had hardened it into something very like papier mâché. She prodded it gently with tweezers, and it responded with all the pliancy of driftwood.

She should, she supposed, count her blessings: this treasure had survived, when it could easily have disintegrated altogether. But why did the process of retrieving anything from the distant past always have to be making the best of a bad job? Why couldn't anything spring from antiquity fresh and intact? Why must all documents be blemished and brittle, all vases broken, all skeletons incomplete, all bracelets rusted, all statues vandalised? Why should only tiny scraps of Sappho's poetry survive — why not *all* of it, or none?

She chewed her fingernails, knowing her irritability was really just nervousness: excitement about what she might disclose, fear that she'd bungle the job. She threw on her jacket and went out to the garage near the railway station and bought four different chocolate bars. By the time she returned to her hotel room, she'd already eaten three of them and her pockets were crackling with the wrappers. She paused in the doorway of her bedroom to take a long swig of complimentary mineral water. Then, highly alert and faintly nauseous, she laid out the tools and equipment for her surgery.

By 3 a.m., she was nudging the confession of Thomas Peirson into the light of the 21st century. For hours, she'd been humidifying the scroll, rolling it gently back and forth on a metal grid suspended over a photographic tray of warm water, then re-sealing it inside a garish placenta of blue plastic. The paper had finally absorbed enough vapour to relax a little, and the gelatine was loosening its grip. Now, with a palette knife, Siân began peeling the outermost sheet from its companions.

Confession of Thos. Peirson, in the Year of Our Lord 1788
In the full and certain Knowledge that my Time is nigh,
for my good Wife has even now closed the door on Doctor
Cubitt & weeps in the room below, I write these words.

The fibres of the paper were exceptionally frail; the rags from which the paper had been made must have been shabby stuff indeed, poorly pounded. The brown ink of Thomas Peirson's handwriting stood out tolerably well against a background that hadn't discoloured much, but then the paper's whiteness had less to do with thorough washing of the rags than with an expedient douse in that brand-new invention (well, brand-new in 1788, anyway) chlorine bleach. Inevitably, the bleach had left its own acid legacy, and with every gentle nudge of Siân's knife, the weakened grain of the humid surface threatened to disintegrate. The words themselves were fragile, the gallic acid and iron sulphate in the brown ink having corroded little holes in the 'e's and 'o's.

below, I write these words. In my fifty years of life I have been

Been what? A thread of the paper had come loose, damaging the crown of one of the words in the line below. Siân paused, dabbed her eyes with her sleeve. She ought to give the paper longer to relax, get some sleep while it did so.

Outside in the street, a drunken male voice shouted an ancient word of contentious etymology, and a female voice responded with laughter. The act from which all humans originate, evoked in a word whose own origins were long lost.

Siân laid her head against her pillow, one leg hanging off the bed, the other twitching wearily on the mattress. She closed her eyes for just a moment, to moisten them before getting back to the task.

'I love you — you must believe that,' the man with the big hands whispered into her ear. 'I'll risk my soul to save yours.'

He sounded so sincere, so overwhelmed by his love for her, that she pressed her cheek against his shoulder and hugged him tight, determined never to be disjoined from him.

Within minutes, of course (or was it hours?), her head was disjoined from her neck, and the seagulls were screaming.

Later that same morning, when the sun was high over Church Street and the hundred and ninety-nine steps were glowing all the way up the East Cliff, Siân stood poised at the foot of them, breathing deeply, getting ready for the climb. The sharpness of the sea air was sort of restorative and yet it was making her dizzy too, and she was finding it hard to decide if she should keep breathing deeply or cut her losses and get moving. She still hadn't begun the climb when, half a dozen breaths later, she was jolted from her under-slept stupor by the shout:

'Kill, Hadrian, kill!'

It was Magnus's voice ringing out, mock-imperious, but she couldn't see where it was coming from. All she knew was that a large animal, barking raucously, fangs bared, had sprung into her path, ready to knock her sprawling.

'Hey!' she yelped, half in fear, half in recognition. Hadrian leapt back on to his haunches, panting with pleasure. His cream-coloured snout was still twitching, his teeth still bared, but in a whimpery, goofy grin.

'Show 'er no mercy, boy,' said Mack, jogging into view. He was taller and better-looking than she remembered, stripped down once again to athletic essentials, his bare legs glistening in the sun, his T-shirt stained with a long spearhead of sweat pointing downwards.

'You scared me,' she chided him, as he drew abreast of her and continued to jog on the spot, his limbs in constant motion.

'Sorry. Cruel sense of humour. Blame it on my father.'

Though his face was flushed and she was regarding his pounding feet and pumping fists with disdainful bemusement, he seemed unable to stop running on the spot. It was an addiction, she'd read somewhere. Exercise junkies.

'For goodness' sake, stand still.'

'It's a glorious day!' he retorted, throwing his arms wide to the sun as he continued to pound the stone under his feet. 'Come on, let's run up the steps!'

'Be my guest,' she said.

'No, together!' He leapt onto the first step, sending Hadrian bounding ahead in a fit of joy; then after scaling a few more, he ran back down to her.

'Come on – show me how fit you are!'

Siân was sick with embarrassment, dumbstruck by

his rudeness. If he noticed her distress, it only spurred him on.

'Come on — slim young woman like you,' he panted, 'should be able to run up a few stairs.'

'Please, Mack . . .' His flattery was crueller than insults. 'Don't do this.'

'It's all about pacing yourself,' he persisted, his face flame-red now, suggesting he was ashamed, but had gone too far to retreat now. 'You take a breath . . . every three stairs . . . sixty-six breaths . . .'

'Mack,' she said. 'I'm an amputee.'

For a moment he paced on, then abruptly stopped.

'Christ,' he said, his fists dangling loose at his sides. 'I'm sorry.'

Hadrian had scampered down to join them again, bearing no grudge for the way they'd teased him. He looked up at Siân and his master's faces, back and forth, as if to say, *What next?*

Mack wiped his huge palm across his face, then did a more thorough job with the hem of his T-shirt. A little boy finding a pretext for hiding his face from an angry parent. A beautiful young man baring his abdomen, muscled like a Greek statue.

You bastard, thought Siân. *I want, I want, I want.*

'Which leg?' asked Mack, when he'd recovered himself.

She lifted her left leg, wiggled it in the air for as long as she could keep her balance.

'It's a good prosthesis,' he said, adopting his best physicianly tone.

'No it's *not*,' she retorted irritably. 'It's a Russian job, mostly wood. Weighs a ton.'

'You haven't considered upgrading to a plastic one? They're really light, and nowadays—'

'Magnus,' she warned him, caught between bewildered laughter and bitter fury, 'it's none of your business.'

To her relief, he dropped the subject, swallowing hard on his no doubt encyclopaedic knowledge of artificial limbs — if 'encyclopaedic' was the correct word for a professional acquaintance with the glossy promotional brochures that prosthetics companies sent to doctors.

'I'm sorry,' he said, sounding genuinely chastened. Hadrian, impatient for action, fidgeted between them, his downy black forehead wrinkled in supplication. Siân stroked him, and it felt good, so she knelt down and stroked him some more.

Mack knelt too, and since her hand was busy with the head and mane, he stroked the flank, hoping she wouldn't pull away.

'How did you lose your leg?' he said gently, not like a doctor quizzing a patient, but like an average person humbled by curiosity to know the gory details.

Siân sighed, not angry with him anymore, but

struck by how absurdly inappropriate the verb 'lose' was in this context, how coy and, at the same time, judgemental. As if she had absentmindedly left her leg on a bus, and it was still lying unclaimed in a lost property office somewhere. As if, when the pain inside her was ready for the kill, she would 'lose' her life like an umbrella.

'I lost it in Bosnia,' she said.

He was instantly impressed. 'In the war?' he suggested. She knew he was picturing her doing something exotically heroic, like pulling wounded children out of burning wreckage, and being blown up by an enemy shell.

'Yes, but it had nothing to do with the war, really,' she said. 'I was there because my boyfriend was a journalist. And we were stepping out of a bar in Gorazde when a car knocked me down, right there on the footpath. It was a drunk teenager behind the wheel.' She frowned irritably at Mack's look of disbelief. 'They have drunk teenagers everywhere, you know, even in Bosnia, even during wars.'

'And your boyfriend?'

'What about my boyfriend?'

'Was he . . . injured?'

'He was killed—'

'—I'm so sorry—'

'—four weeks later, by sniper fire. He'd already dumped me by then. Said he just couldn't see it working out, him and a disabled person. He'd have to devote his whole life to taking care of me, he thought.'

Mack grimaced, tarred with the guilt of a fellow male he'd never even met.

'You've done brilliantly, though,' he said.

'Thank you.'

'No one would know.'

'Not unless they tried to make me run up a hundred and ninety-nine steps, no.'

'I'm really sorry.'

Siân patted Hadrian's head. It was as far as she was willing to go towards letting the dog's master off the hook. *Let him sweat*, she thought. Metaphorically speaking, of course. Every muscle on his torso seemed already to be defined with the stuff.

'Speaking of contrition...' she said. 'Your message in a bottle ... your confession ...'

'Yes?' He seized the change of subject gratefully, his head cocked in deference.

'The job is trickier than I thought. You're going to have to decide what's more important to you, Mack: knowing what that document says, or keeping it the way you like it. The shape of it, I mean. If I succeed in peeling those pages apart, I'll be doing well. I can't give them back to you in the form of a nice tight scroll inside a bottle.'

'So what are you suggesting?'

'I'm not suggesting anything,' she said, manoeuvring him gently towards where she wanted him. 'It's *your* heirloom, Mack. I can glue the bottle shut again, return it to you tomorrow.'

She turned away to acknowledge Michael coming up the steps, greeting the poor little duffer with a cheery wave. Michael nodded back, squinting, almost tripping over his own feet in his attempt not to intrude. She could tell that in his myopic eyes, she and Mack were the enigma of romance, stumbled upon, unearthed, only to be handed over to experts for analysis. Sweet, shy little man — how she despised him ...

'I don't know,' Mack was saying. 'There's something magic about it, just the way it is ...'

'Well, there *is* one thing we could do,' she said, figuring she'd softened him up enough. 'I could make you a new scroll out of papier mâché, and stick a facsimile of the outermost page on the outside. I know how to make things like that look old and authentic. The original papers could be mounted on board, preserved properly, and you could have a replica that'd look pretty close to what your dad found.'

He laughed.

'More historical fakery, eh?'

She looked him square in the eyes.

'Do you want to know what the confession says or not?'

He pondered for no longer than three seconds. 'I do,' he conceded.

That afternoon, Siân and her colleagues at the dig said goodbye to Keira and Trevor, who were decamping to the Middle East. In their place, the 'very nice people' from north Wales had already settled in — another married couple who'd been together forever. They wore matching jumpers and identical shoes. They whispered to each other as they worked, and kissed each other on the shoulder or on the side of the head. Siân knew very well they were adorable, but disliked them with an irrational passion. They smelled so strongly of happiness that even on the exposed headland of Whitby's East Cliff, the odour was overpowering.

I want, I want, I want.

At three-thirty, the heavens opened and the site supervisor declared the day's digging at an end. Thirteen of the fourteen archaeologists hurriedly dispersed into the downpour, hunched under nylon hoods and plastic habits, like a herd of monks fleeing a new Dissolution of the Monasteries. The younger ones sprinted down towards the town, free to embrace the unimaginable luxuries of the modern world.

Siân, without a raincoat or umbrella, walked gingerly on the slick and treacherous terrain, watching where she put her feet as the rain penetrated her scalp and trickled down the back of her neck.

Every few seconds, she cast a glance towards the hundred and ninety-nine steps, hoping against hope that Mack and Hadrian would be coming up to meet her. They weren't, of course. Still she cherished a forlorn fantasy of Mack surfacing from the horizon, running up the steps, one arm holding aloft an umbrella. Pathetic. Saint Hilda would be shaking her head despairingly, if she knew.

The car-park between the abbey ruins and Saint Mary's Church, which ordinarily failed to register on Siân's consciousness at all, annoyed her intensely today as she crossed it. What was it doing here, littering a sacred space with automotive junk? Buried somewhere underneath this dismal moat of concrete, this petrol-stained eyesore, lay oratories and other buildings erected by simple Christians more than a thousand years ago. What would it take to clear away this garbage, short of a bomb?

Siân winced at a flash of recollection — the sound of the shelling she'd experienced in Bosnia, the blasts and rumbles that drove her deeper into the crook of Patrick's arm as they lay in bed, a few miles from the action.

'Pretend it's a thunderstorm,' he'd advised her. 'It can't hurt you.'

'Unless it hits you,' she'd said.

'Then you won't feel anything,' he'd said, almost asleep.

A lie, of course. Nothing dies painlessly. Even a limb that's long gone keeps hurting.

For more than an hour, Siân traipsed around the streets of Whitby, searching for something to eat. She was in one of those perverse moods where nothing seemed appealing except what was patently not on offer. A lively Greek or Turkish restaurant, with lots of different dips and delicacies and peasant waiters hollering at each other across the room — that would do. Or a Chinese buffet, with spiced noodles and tiny spring rolls and hot soup. She was most definitely not in the mood for fish and chips, which, in Whitby, was an unfortunate way to be.

Window after window, street after street, she peered through foggy panes of glass and read menus that offered her cod and potato in its various disguises, served with mushy peas, pickled egg, curry sauce, gravy. A sign on the front door of the Plough Inn said 'Sorry, no food today'. A bistro that looked promising wasn't open till the evening. The Tandoori place near the station was good, but she'd eaten there yesterday, and besides, she wanted something instantly.

She ended up eating a banana-and-ice-cream crêpe in a café across the river. They served it with the ice-cream folded inside the pancake rather than on top, so the whole thing was already a lukewarm mess even as she made the first incision with her toothless knife. Chasing the disappearing warmth, she ate too fast, then felt sick.

If she'd been one of Saint Hilda's nuns, she reflected, she would have dined on bread and wine, in the company of friends. She would have drawn a circle in the air and someone would have silently handed her something wholesome, and there wouldn't have been this Top Forty gibberish blaring into her ears.

Dream on, dream on.

She paid for her pancake and crossed the bridge to her hotel, still haunted, to top it all off, by the fantasy of Magnus cresting the horizon with an umbrella held aloft.

Siân's nightmare next morning was an ingenious variant on the usual. In this version, she had just a few precious seconds to find where her severed head had rolled and replace it on her neck, before the quivering nerves and arteries lost their ability to reunite. Her consciousness seemed to be floating somewhere between the two, powerless to guide her headless body as it groped and fumbled on the floor, its gory neck densely packed with what looked like gasping, sucking macaroni. Her head lay near the open door, inches from the steep stairwell, its eyes fluttering, its lips dry, licked by an anxious tongue. With a bump, Siân woke up on the floor next to her bed.

I really am losing my mind, she thought.

Still, looking on the bright side, she'd slept quite well, and for an uncommonly long stretch of hours. Buttery-yellow sunlight was beaming through the velux window, flickering gently as seagulls wheeled over the roof. The screaming was over, and breakfast would be served downstairs. Most cheeringly of all, she'd made good progress last night on Thomas Peirson's confession.

Before going to bed, she'd managed to liberate the whole of the outermost page. Aside from those 'o's and 'e's already lost to the corrosive ink, there'd been no further mishaps; she'd proceeded with the utmost gentleness, ignoring the pangs of indigestion and . . . and whatever that lump in her left thigh might be. The lump was more palpable and more painful all the time, but she refused to let it terrorise her. She'd made a solemn vow, when she'd finally walked out of that hospital in Belgrade, feeling each clumsy step reverberating through the cushioned mould of her prosthesis, that she would never lie in a hospital bed again, ever. She would keep that vow. And if she was condemned to die soon, at least she'd die knowing she'd done a good job on this confession.

A hastily scribbled transcript of what she'd unwrapped so far was lying on the spare pillow of her double bed. Pity it had to be written on a cheap little notepad with a *Star Wars* actress on the cover, but that was the only writing paper to hand last night, and she was so impatient to share Thomas Peirson's secrets with Mack that she simply couldn't wait. He would be in seventh heaven when he saw this. He was just the sort of guy who'd be keen on murder mysteries, she could tell.

She scooped yesterday's skirt off the floor and held it up to the sunlight. It was well and truly ripe for the laundromat; she would wear something fresh today. To celebrate the first page.

All the way to work, the cheap little *Star Wars* notepad burned a hole in Siân's jacket pocket, and her ears were cocked for the sound of Mack's voice, or the heavy breathing of Hadrian. Neither sound came to her, however, and she joined her colleagues at the dig, tilling the soil for human remains.

At lunch-time, she wandered down to the kiosk and had a peek out into the world beyond the abbey grounds. Nothing. She considered going down to Loggerhead's Yard and actually visiting Mack at his house, but that didn't feel right.

After all, he might kill me, she thought — then blinked in surprise at the idea. What a thing to think! Nevertheless, she'd rather wait until he came to her.

She strolled back to the abbey remains. The fine lunch-time weather was luring visitors to the site — not just tourists, but also the children of English

Heritage staff. Bobby and Jemima, the son and daughter of one of the kiosk workers, were running around the ruins, shrieking with laughter. At seven and six years old respectively, they weren't worried that their scrambling feet would erode the stonework of the pedestal stubs littering the grassy nave. They were so young, in fact, that they could even kiss each other without worrying about the consequences.

'Hi, Bobby! Hi, Jemima!' called Siân, waving.

The children were mucking about near the vanished sacristy, lying down flat and jumping up in turn, pirouetting gracelessly.

'What are you doing?' said Siân.

Jemima was swaying on her feet, dizzy after another spin; Bobby was lying in a peculiar hollowed-out depression in a rectangle of stone, staring up at the sky.

'We're tryin' to see the wumman jumpin',' he explained.

'What woman?'

'The ghostie wumman that jumps off the top.' Bobby pointed, and Siân followed the line of his grubby finger to the roofless buttresses of the abbey. 'You spin three times, then you lie in the grave, then you see her.'

'Have you seen her?' said Siân.

'Nah,' said Jemima. 'We've not spinned 'ard enough.'

And the two of them ran off, laughing.

Siân looked down at the hollow in the stone, wondering what it used to be before it served as a toy sarcophagus for superstitious children. Then she peered up at the abbey buttresses, imagining a woman moving along them, a young woman in a flowing white gown, her bare feet treading the stone tightrope with all the sureness of a sleepwalker.

'*HUSH!*'

Siân almost jumped out of her skin as the dog shouted his greeting right next to her. She staggered off-balance, and did a little dance to regain her footing, much to Hadrian's delight.

'Honestly, Hadrian,' she scolded him. 'Who taught you *that* trick?'

'My dad, I suppose,' said Mack, ambling up behind. He was dressed in black denim trousers and a grey Nike sweatshirt with the sleeves gathered up to his elbows; he looked better than ever.

'That's right, blame the departed,' said Siân.

'But it's *true*,' he protested. 'I'm just a foster carer, stuck with a delinquent orphan. Aren't I, Hadrian, eh?' And he patted the dog vigorously on the back, almost slapping him.

'You didn't need to pay £1.70 to meet me,' said Siân. 'I would've come out eventually.'

He laughed. 'Sod that. I want to know what that confession says.'

'One page a day is the best I can manage,' she cautioned him.

'I'll take what I can get.'

She pulled the notebook from her jacket pocket, flipped Princess Whatsername over and immediately began to read aloud:

Confession of Thos. Peirson, in the Year of Our Lord 1788

In the full and certain Knowledge that my Time is nigh, for my good Wife has even now closed the door on Doctor Cubitt & weeps in the room below, I write these words. In my fifty years of Life I have been a Whaler and latterly an Oil Merchant; to my family I have given such comforts as have been allow'd me, and to God I have given what I could in thanks. All who know me, know me as a man who means harm to no one.

Yet, as I prepare to meet my Maker, there is but one memory He sets afore me; one dreddeful scene He bids me live again. My hands, though cold now with Fever, do seem to grow warm, from the flesh of <u>her</u> neck — my beloved Mary. Such a slender neck it was, without flaw, fitting inside my big hands like a coil of anchor rope.

I meant, at first, no more than to strangle her — to put such marks upon her throat as could not be mistaken. Despoiled tho' she was, I was loath to despoil her more; I would do only so much as would spare her the wrath of the townsfolk, and secure her repose among the Blessed. So, I resolved only to strangle her. But

She looked up at him.

'But?' he prompted.

'That's it, so far. A page-and-a-bit.'

Mack tilted his head back, narrowed his eyes in concentration.

'Maybe he thought she was a vampire,' he suggested after a minute. 'Maybe he strangled her while she was sleeping, thinking she was going to sprout fangs when the sun came up.'

'I don't think so,' sighed Siân.

'Well, Whitby is the town of Dracula, isn't it?'

'Not in 1788,' she said, restraining herself from a more fulsome put-down.

'I know damn well when the novel was written,' he growled. 'But maybe Bram Stoker was — what's the word? — *inspired* by how everybody in Whitby was vampire-mad.'

'I don't think so. I think the people of Whitby were worried about their menfolk drowning in the North Sea, not about Transylvanian bloodsuckers running around in black capes.'

'They were pretty superstitious, though, weren't they, these 18th-century Yorkshire people?'

'I wasn't alive then, believe it or not. But I think we can be pretty sure our man Thomas Peirson, if he strangled someone, wasn't doing it because of a story that hadn't been written yet by a novelist who wasn't even born here.'

64

Mack's eyes went a bit glazed as something came back to him. 'My dad showed me Count Dracula's grave once, in Saint Mary's churchyard. I must have been six.'

'Naughty man. Were you scared?'

'Bloody terrified; I had nightmares for days. I adored it, though. Nothing more thrilling than fear, is there?'

She looked down uneasily. 'I don't know about that.'

'OK, maybe *one* thing,' he conceded. His voice was soft, deep, good-humoured; the tint of bawdiness in it was unmistakable.

'Tell you what,' said Siân, blushing. 'Why don't you show me the grave?'

The East Cliff churchyard may have been the final earthly resting place for hundreds of humans, but for Hadrian this grassy expanse of headland was Heaven. He dashed across the green, leaping over tombstones as if they were sporting hurdles provided especially for him, rather like those handsome black receptacles on the seashore embossed *DOG WASTE*. With such a huge playground to explore, he was quite content to let his master and mistress get on with whatever they were here for.

'I don't know if I can find it, after so many years,' said Mack, shielding his eyes under the visor of his massive right hand.

'Put yourself back in that little boy's shoes,' she suggested.

He laughed, and lifted up one Size 12 foot. 'You've got to be joking.'

They both, at exactly the same time, recalled the moment when she'd lifted her prosthetic leg for him on the hundred and ninety-nine steps. The moment when the scales fell from his eyes, and she knew with perfect certainty that he was imagining her body and wondering how he'd feel about it if it were stretched out naked beside him.

He reached out to her, cupped her shoulder in his palm.

'Look, it's all right,' he said.

She walked ahead of him, face turned away.

'Lots and lots of these graves are empty, did you know that?' she declared, in a brisk, informative tone. 'Sailors would be lost at sea, and the families would have a funeral, put up a headstone . . .'

'Ah, historical fakery again . . .'

'Not at all. It preserves a different kind of history — the reality of the loved ones' grief.'

He hummed dubiously. 'I'm not a grief kinda guy, Siân. Bury the dead, get on with living, that's my motto.'

She shivered without knowing why. She couldn't remember if he'd ever spoken her name before today. The way he voiced it, exhaled it at leisure over his tongue, 'Siân' sounded like a noise of satisfaction.

They wandered around for another five minutes or so, but failed to find the unmarked grave Mack's father had told him was Dracula's. What they did find was something Siân had read about in a book: an adjacent pair of gravestones — one oval and flat to the ground, the other a tiny upright miniature — which countless generations of children had been assured marked the graves of Humpty Dumpty and Tom Thumb.

'My dad never told me that,' said Mack.

'Well there you are: another black mark against him.'

They went to fetch Hadrian, who was merrily digging up clods of earth all over the place. Siân glanced at the weathered tombstones as she walked, reading the odd name here and there if it was still legible. Sea-spray and the wind of centuries had erased the finer details, and she wasn't in the mood to study the stones closely, as she was getting peckish. But suddenly she did a double-take and stumbled backwards.

'It's our man!' she cried. 'Mack! It's our man!'

He bounded to her side — him and Hadrian both. Standing somewhat skew-whiff on the ground before them was a tall headstone clearly inscribed THOMAS PEIRSON, WHALER AND OIL MERCHANT. According to the remainder of the text, he was the husband of Catherine, father of Anne and Illegible. He died, as he'd anticipated in his confession, in 1788, but there was no hint of him having done anything to warrant remorse. Not so much as a 'God have mercy on his soul'.

The discovery of Peirson's headstone galvanised Mack, sending him sniffing around the other graves, squinting at the inscriptions. It was as if it hadn't occurred to him before now that his treasure-in-a-bottle was something more than a bizarre relic — that it was still intimately connected with the world at large.

'I wonder if his victim's here, too?' he was muttering, as he moved from grave to grave. 'Mary... Mary... If only she'd had a more unusual first name...' He bent down to peer at an epitaph, reciting the bits he considered interesting. '"... in the thirty-fourth year of her age..." No cause of death listed, though... Shame...'

There was something about his attitude that Siân found provocative.

'Well, Doctor Magnus, this *is* a churchyard, not a hospital mortuary. These headstones are commemorations, they're not here to satisfy your curiosity.'

'What do you mean, *my* curiosity?' he retorted, stung. 'Of the two of us, who's digging up dead bodies, poking around in people's bones?'

Siân turned on her heel, and began to walk away.

How instinctively, how helplessly they argued with each other! The last person she'd argued with so much, she ended up declaring her undying love to — not to mention following him to a war zone and shielding him from the impact of an oncoming car. There was no hope for her; she was doomed.

'Let's not make a big thing of this,' he said, catching up to her. 'Can I take you out to lunch?'

She tried to say no, but Hadrian was at her side now, rubbing his downy snout against her skirt as she walked, snuffling in anticipation of her touch. She allowed her hand to fall into his mane, felt his skull arching against her palm. Her stomach rumbled.

'We could have a cup of tea at The Mission,' she said. 'They let dogs in there.'

'The Mission?'

'The Whitby Mission and Seafarer's Centre. They run a coffee shop.'

'Don't be silly — I'll drop Hadrian off at home and take you to a proper restaurant.'

Determined not to argue, she said, 'OK, then: Indian.'

But his brow wrinkled into a frown. 'Let me think...'

'What's wrong with Indian?'

'I'd rather something more...um...unusual.'

She took a deep breath as they began to descend the hundred and ninety-nine steps.

'From a historical point of view,' she said, trying to convince herself she wasn't arguing but only making an interesting observation, 'you surely can't get much more unusual than Punjabi food in a Northumbrian fishing town.'

'*You* know what I mean,' he said. 'The small-town Indian restaurant . . . it's so . . . provincial.'

'Well, we're in a *province*, for goodness' sake!' she snapped. 'We're not in London now.'

'Wow,' he said. 'You're the only person I know who says "for goodness' sake", even when she looks ready to clock me one.'

'So? Does that make me cute?'

'Yes, it makes you cute. And by the way, you're dressed very nicely today. You're looking fantastic.'

Siân felt herself colouring from the hairline down. As his compliment sank in, so did the realisation that, God help her, she really *had* dressed and groomed herself with unusual care this morning. Her skirt, tights and boots were classy co-ordinates and, as her blush travelled further down her body, she was reminded that the neckline of the top she'd chosen was, for the first time in years, low enough to show off her collarbones.

'Uh . . . look,' she said, only a few steps shy of Church Street, 'I've just realised: I don't have time to go to a restaurant. I'm supposed to be back at work in five minutes.'

He stared at her, mouth open, clearly and sincerely disappointed.

'This evening, then.'

She thought fast; there was a tightness in her throat, like hands pressing on her neck. 'I'm going to be working on the next page of your confession this evening,' she said breathlessly.

For a few moments they stood there, eye to eye. Then he smiled, dropped his gaze down to his shoes in good-humoured defeat, and let her go.

'Another time,' he said, as he stepped onto the cobbled street and motioned Hadrian to accompany him into the town. Hadrian looked around once at Siân, then trotted to join his foster-carer in a fast-flowing stream of tourists, native Northumbrians, and less adorable dogs.

In Siân's dream next morning, there was, for a change, no knife. The man was cradling her in his arms, both his hands safely accounted for, one supporting her back, the other stroking her hair. It wasn't what you'd call a happy dream, though: her hair felt wet, slick with a shampoo-like substance which she realised after a while was her own blood. In fact, she was covered in it, and so was he.

'I will carry you up the hundred and ninety-nine steps,' he was crooning to her, in a broken voice. His eyes were almost incandescent with love and grief, and there were droplets of blood twinkling on his eyebrows. He looked like Magnus, except he wasn't. 'I will carry you up the hundred and ninety-nine steps,' he kept promising.

She tried to speak, to reassure him she understood why he had done what he had done, but her windpipe blew blood bubbles, and her tongue was growing stiff.

No particular climactic event woke her, only thirst and a pressing need to go to the loo. She'd drunk half a bottle of wine last night, to kill the pain in her 'innermost parts', and it seemed to have done the trick: her headache was so bad she wasn't aware of the lump in her thigh at all.

Her hair felt tacky, and smelled of alcohol; she washed it in the bathroom sink, half-expecting the water to run crimson. The veins in her temples went *whumpa whumpa whumpa* as she rinsed the shampoo out and groped for a towel. Only then did it occur to her that she may have been sozzled when she was working on the confession.

The second page was still lying on the table, pressed flat under a rectangle of transparent plastic. She examined the wrinkled leaf of paper and the curlicues of ink closely, anxiously. As far as she could tell, there was no damage that hadn't already been done before she came along.

Next she consulted the little *Star Wars* notebook in

which she'd jotted the transcript. It was perfectly lucid — neater, if anything, than her handwriting tended to be when she was stone-cold sober.

She wandered back to the bathroom to dry and style her hair.

At lunch-time, in the same West Side café where she'd made herself sick on pancake, Siân read aloud from her little notebook while Mack listened intently. He leaned very close to her, his cheek almost brushing her shoulder, but then it was quite noisy in the café, as the staff and other customers were watching American soap operas on an elevated TV.

'So, I resolved only to strangle her,' she declaimed, while third-rate actors spat fake bile at each other overhead.

But, God help me, my thumbes became weak, & made no mark upon her flesh, or none that did not fade straightway afterward. These same hands, which have slashed deep into the hide of a Whale, which have lifted barrels heavier than a man; these hands which, even in my latter years of feebleness, could cleave a log in twain with a single ax blow — these hands could not put upon her pale and tender neck the bruises that would save her. I fancied I could hear her voice, already condemn'd to inhabit the wilds of Perdition, crying to me, imploring me to act afore the alarum be raised, and she be found, naked and ripe for Damnation. Nothing, only I, stood betwixt her helpless soul and the worst of Fates. I did

but pause to cover her with a blanket, then hurried to fetch
my knife

Siân put the notepad down, lifted her coffee-cup to her lips.

'Wow,' said Mack, grinning broadly. 'Talk about *coitus interruptus . . .*'

She sipped the hot brew, troubled by her inability to judge the aptness — or offensiveness — of this remark. Seen in one light, it was a flash of wit only a prude would object to (and after all, he *was* a doctor), but in another light, it was gruesomely, outrageously off. From one light to another she veered, and the moment passed, and she was silent. With Patrick, too, she'd become unable to stop her morality dispersing into his.

'You know what we should do?' he said, stabbing his fork into a wodge of chocolate cake. 'We should sell this story to the press.'

We? she thought, before replying: 'The press? What press? The *Whitby Gazette*?' Only a few minutes before, he'd been leafing through the café's free papers, chortling, in his smug London way, at local place names like Fryup, and inventing preposterous news stories for the *Gazette*, such as an outbreak of psittacosis amongst homing pigeons. 'Chief Inspector Beaver is investigating claims that the deadly bacterium was purchased from an unscrupulous doctor,' he'd intoned, poker-faced, 'by Mister Ee-Bah-Goom of the Whitby Flying Club, as part of a cunning plan to employ germ warfare against his rivals.' She'd laughed despite herself.

'You do think small, don't you?' he gently disparaged her now. 'I'm thinking of a big colour feature in one of the major national supplements — *The Sunday Times*, maybe, or the *Telegraph*.'

She was pricked to anger by his condescension; she felt that, after all she'd seen at Patrick's side, she wasn't a total innocent in the big bad world of newspapers.

'Do you think they care? Look at the way they've ignored our dig at the abbey! To get a major newspaper interested nowadays, you virtually have to dig up King Arthur's round table, or a previously unknown play by Shakespeare.'

'Not at all. This is murder. Murder sells.'

She knew he was right, but felt compelled to keep arguing anyway. The thought of her beautiful 18th-century manuscript, which she was so lovingly unpeeling from itself, being splashed across the pages of a throwaway Sunday supplement, made her sick.

'It's a very, very out-of-date murder,' she said, hoping a cynical, jocular tone would score with him. 'Way past its use-by date.'

He laughed, and leaned across the table, staring straight into her eyes.

'Murder never goes off,' he said, and, leaning further still, he kissed her on the cheek, right near the edge of her lips.

Siân closed her eyes, praying for guidance as to how to respond. Slapping his face would be so frightfully old-fashioned, and besides, she was afraid of him, and also, it might spoil her only chance of happiness before the cancer decided that her time was up.

'Hadrian will be getting lonely,' she said. 'You'd better go and rescue him.'

That afternoon, Siân left the dig early, telling Nina she thought she might be coming down with 'flu.

Nina scrutinised her face and said, 'Yes, you don't look well at all,' which was rather discouraging, since the 'flu story was a lie. In reality, the lump in Siân's thigh was so painful she could barely work, and she was hoping that if she stopped kneeling at her appointed excavation and putting so much pressure on her stump hour after hour, the pain might ease off.

'I'm getting a sore throat myself,' said Nina. 'Let's hope it's not the Black Death, eh?'

Siân walked stiffly back into town. Her whole pelvis was aching: a subtle network of pain radiating, it seemed, from the lump inwards. A kernel of malignancy haloed with roots and tendrils, like a potato left too long in a cupboard, silently mutating in the dark. Fibrosis. Metastasis. Dissemination. Words only a doctor should be intimately familiar with.

On her way to the White Horse and Griffin, she bought a bottle of brandy, a box of painkillers and, as an afterthought, a king-size block of chocolate. In the privacy of her hotel room, she consumed some of each, at regular intervals, while working on the next page of Thomas Peirson's secret testament.

'OK,' said Mack the following day, leaning forward expectantly. 'Carry on where we left off, yes?'

'Yes.' She took a long deep breath, filling her lungs with sea air.

She'd arranged to meet him half-way up the hundred and ninety-nine steps, on the same bench where they'd first sat together. It was more convenient than a café or a restaurant; she wouldn't have so far to walk back to the dig, and she was quite content to eat the apple she'd pocketed that morning in the hotel's breakfast room. Fruit was probably quite a sensible thing to lunch on after a hangover, and she'd already promised herself that chocolate would never again pass her lips — in *either* direction.

Also, it was brilliant sunny weather today, and being out in the fresh air meant that Hadrian could be here with them, and she'd missed Hadrian so badly yesterday.

Also, Mack was less likely, she imagined, to kiss her on a public thoroughfare. Thus postponing the inevitable.

'*I did but pause to cover her with a blanket, then hurried to fetch my knife,*' recited Siân from her little notebook. Hadrian promptly laid a mendicant paw on her knee — the right knee, the one that was flesh and blood — to alert her to the fact she'd stopped stroking him. 'Oh, Hadrian, I'm sorry,' she crooned, ruffling his mane. 'What a *bad* mother I am . . .'

'Come on, come on,' growled Mack impatiently. 'He'll survive. *Read.*'

She raised the notebook, savouring her modicum of power over him — the only power she had left, before she surrendered completely.

I did but pause to cover her with a blanket, then hurried to fetch my knife — that same knife I have used for a thousand innocent purposes — cutting rope, gipping fish, paring fruit, carving blubber. Believing myself to be alone in the house, I came down the stairs without caution, and was surpriz'd by our Anne in the parlour, crying, Father, what is the matter? Go catch your Mother up at market, I says. We are not needing a ham after all, for I mind now that Butcher Finch said he would give us one in lieu of payment for his oil. So she runs off, God bless her.

I found my knife, and returned to the room upstairs — the same room where I now write these words. It seemed to

me that Mary had moved away from where I put her down —
crawled towards the door — but when I spoke her name, she
lay still. Once more I gathered her close to my breast,
cradling her like a bairn. How I yearned to spare her the
knife! Had I the nerve to beat her black and blew instead, to
stave in her soft skull with my fists, and splinter her ribs like
kindling? I owned I had not. So, without pausing any more,
I lowered her into the wash-copper, and hewed the blade
deep into her neck, cleaving her flesh to the bone. Her blood
flowed out like a wave, like a wave of shining crimson,
clothing her nakedness.

Siân looked up. Mack's eyes were bright with excitement, his great hands clasped white-knuckled against
his chin. In her eagerness to bring him the latest
instalment, she must surely have known he'd respond
like this, but now that she saw that look in his eyes, she
felt ashamed.

'That's all,' she said, with an awkward smile.
'That's all I could get done. If you knew what it
took . . .'

He leaned back, letting it all sink in. 'Wow,' he
sighed. 'This guy was a genuine, authentic 18th-
century psycho. Hannibal Lecter in a frilly shirt.'

'Who's Hannibal Lecter?'

'Come on! The world's favourite serial killer! You
mean you've never seen *The Silence of the Lambs*?'

'Lovely title,' she said, responding to Hadrian's

urgent pleas for stroking at last. 'Sounds like a Pre-Raphaelite painting by William Holman Hunt or someone like that.'

'Who's William Holman Hunt?'

They sat in silence for a few seconds, while Siân petted Hadrian and Mack watched the dog go demented in her hands.

'Anyway, our man Thomas Peirson,' he declared, when finally, to his bemusement, Siân's face disappeared in Hadrian's flank. 'He's a star, can't you see? He could really put Whitby on the map — the *modern* map.'

Siân surfaced, blinking.

'Don't you ever get tired,' she challenged him, 'of this ever-so-*modern* fascination with psychopaths and sick deeds? It can't be good for us — as a culture, I mean. Filling ourselves up with madness and cruelty.'

'Face it, Siân, when was it ever different? Madness and cruelty have always been the staple diet of history.' And he smiled, secure in the knowledge that he had, among many other things, Hitler and De Sade on his side.

Siân looked away from him, towards the headland, for inspiration. 'Think of Saint Hilda founding the original monastery here,' she said, 'long before Whitby was even called Whitby. Think of the devotion, the sheer strength of spirit invested in this place. A little powerhouse of prayer, perched on a clifftop next to a wild sea. I find that thrilling — much more thrilling than serial killers.'

'Jolly good, jolly good,' he said, in a fruity mockery of an upper-class relic. 'But honestly, Siân, I'm sure your Saint Hilda was as twisted as they come.'

Violently, she jerked to face him, startling Hadrian with the sudden movement.

'What would *you* know?' she snapped, as the poor dog cowered between them.

'Oh, I've read plenty,' Magnus shot back. 'Did you know that in the middle of the night, friendly elves drop history books through my letterbox? It's like the Open University, it's amazing what you learn. The complete rundown on religious fanatics in England, with colour illustrations. Step-by-step instructions for flagellating yourself.'

'You're making no effort to understand these people! Just because they weren't driving around in cars, talking into mobile phones . . .'

He threw his hands up, just like Patrick used to do, and exclaimed, 'Christ almighty: the arrogance! You're assuming that if I were only a bit more educated, I'd realise what total *darlings* these lunatics really were. Well, I *have* read my history books and my glossy brochures, thank you very much. And these monks and friars and abbesses, *some* of them may've believed in what they were doing, but their philosophy *stinks*. Hatred of the human body, that's what it

81

boils down to. Hatred of natural desires, hatred of pleasure. Think of their routine, Siân: knocked out of bed at midnight, walk to a horrible gloomy hall, kneel down on a hard floor, start praying in the freezing cold, pray and chant all night and all day. Wear rough clothes specially designed to stop you feeling too comfortable. Nice food forbidden, just in case you're tempted to gluttony. Conversation forbidden, in case it distracts you from being a zombie. And if you dare to break the rules, you get flogged publicly. It's *sick!*'

He pointed up towards the abbey, his thumb and forefinger as rigid as a gun.

'*That's* why those ruins are ruins, can't you see that? It's got nothing to do with hurricanes, or Henry VIII, or German warships taking pot-shots at the abbey in 1914. It's got to do with society growing up – evolving to the point where we realise we don't *need* a bunch of sad old perverts telling us we'll go to Hell if we enjoy life too much. It's the 21st century, Siân, wake up!'

'You're yelling at me,' she said, miserable with *déjà vu*. Screaming rows with Patrick, heads turning in crowded places, furious tussles finally won and lost under rumpled bedsheets.

Magnus folded his arms across his chest and glowered.

'For Christ's sake.' He was making a strenuous

effort to keep his voice down. 'The Dark Ages are over, haven't you noticed? People enjoy taking a peek at the ruins, they'll buy a postcard of Saint Hilda at the kiosk, but that's as far as it goes. Sooner or later, the last few walls will fall down, and it'll be *adios*, ta-ta, good*night*.'

'Those walls,' said Siân frostily, 'will still be standing when people like you are long gone. None of your ... huffing and puffing can change that.'

He glared at her, thrusting his massive shoulders forward as if bracing himself to punch her. Instead, with a groan of frustration, he suddenly threw his arms around her and pulled her close to him, crushing her against his chest.

'You drive me crazy,' he murmured, his breath hot in her ear, his heartbeat pervading her bosom. 'I want you.' And he kissed her full on the mouth.

Siân squirmed, embarrassed for him, loath to reject him so publicly, in front of anyone who might be passing by – and besides, she was aroused, intensely aroused. She pulled her mouth away, but wrapped her arms around his waist, clinging hard, her cheek pressed against his jaw. If they could only hold each other like this, breast to breast, for the rest of her life, it would be enough. Nothing else would need to happen.

He began to stroke the back of her head, one palm smoothing her hair; his hand felt big enough to hold her skull inside it, and she was electrified with fear and desire.

'Give me time,' she whispered – and he let her go.

'All the time . . . in the world,' he reassured her, breathing harder than if he'd just run up and down the steps. 'Just say you'll see me again.'

She laughed shakily, delighted with the high drama of it all, despising it too. Hadrian only made it worse, looking from her to Mack and back again, with that absurd wrinkle-browed *What next?* expression of his.

'Of course,' she said. 'Tomorrow, lunchtime. I'll have the rest of the confession for you.'

'Of course,' he said, perspiring with relief. A semblance of normality settled in the air around them; the world expanded to include passersby on the church stairs, seagulls, the harbour. The town and its environs had held its breath while they were kissing; now it was letting it out.

'Where shall we meet?' said Mack.

Siân thought for a moment.

'The Whitby Mission. They let dogs in there.'

He opened his mouth to argue, then grinned.

'The Whitby Mission.' His right hand, whose warm imprint still tingled on her back, reached down to Hadrian, grabbing the dog by the scruff of the neck. 'They'll let *you* in there, did you hear that?' he announced, pulling the handful of hair teasingly to and fro. 'And we'll find out what that bad man did with the body, eh? Won't that be exciting?'

Hadrian wasn't convinced, baring his teeth and twisting his head in frustrated pursuit of the badgering grip.

'Rough!' he complained.

The inner layers of the scroll were, contrary to Siân's expectations, the most damaged. Something had leaked into them at some stage in their two-hundred-year confinement, something more corrosive than simple moisture or the intrinsic hazards of the gelatine and the ink. Try as she might to peel the pages apart with no damage to the integrity of the fibres or the calligraphy, there were small mishaps along the way: an abrasion of the paper surface here, a comma or a flourish lost to impatience. She took a swig of brandy straight from the bottle, and worked on, sweat trickling into her eyes.

'Come on, you!' she muttered, as she laboured to unfasten, millimetre by millimetre, the page she already knew from the page she hadn't read yet. 'Explain yourself.' There must surely be a reason behind Thomas Peirson's actions, a better reason than mere evil. Decent, godfearing 18th-century men were not psychopaths, plotting their motiveless murders for the future delectation of Hollywood.

But with every word that came to light, Thomas

Peirson's soul emerged darker and more disturbing. Sentence by sentence, he painted himself to be exactly the remorseless monster she'd seen reflected in Mack's excited eyes.

When the deed was done, I was in a frenzy of haste. Mary's body I swaddled in waxed sailcloth and hid in a chest; then I washed clean of blood my self, the copper, the knife, and the floor; whereupon I took my place at table downstairs, affecting to be busy with accounts.

The remainder of that day, and the next day after it, were a torture greater than any I expect to suffer in the Time-To-Come, even if it should please God to banish me from his mercy and cast me to the Devil. While Mary's carcase lay stiffening in my sea-chest, I joined my worried wife and daughter, all throughout the streets of Whitby, searching for our lost lamb. We questioned folk on the East side and the West side; we walked till we were weary.

She has run away with that William Agar, my wife says. He has taken her, the blackguard.

So, we visited William's mother & axed her what she knew, and she replied with such a skriking as set our ears ringing. My boy is gone up to London, she says, and you are deceived if you think he would dream of taking your daft daughter with him. My boy has been fair driven away, to get peace from all her fond stories & her lies — I have had the poor lad beating his brow, saying, Mother, are all girls so cack-brained, to see love where none was ever offered? Now he is free of her mischief at last, and if she means to follow him to London, I pray her wiles get her no farther than a whorehouse in York!

After this exchange, I took Catherine home in a terrible anger, and indeed this gave her a certain courage for a while, but then we fell again to waiting for Mary to come home. Hour upon hour, all three of us strained our ears for the footsteps I knew would not sound. She has come to harm! my dear wife wept, wringing her hands. She has come to harm, I know it! Nonsense, woman, I said, inventing a dozen comforting stories with happy embraces for endings.

On the third night, my family at last took to their beds and slept deep, and I carried my beloved Mary out into the night — being newly in the oil trade then, I had the strength of a whaler yet, & bore her in my arms as easy as a thief bears a sack of candlesticks. Under cover of darkness I ran down the ghaut to the riverside, and there I discharged her poor body into the restless waters.

Next morning, she is found, and fetched up on Fish Pier. The cry of MURDER! spreads throughout the town, from mouth to mouth, until it reaches my door. Still I dissembled — You are mistaken, It cannot be, &c. But then they brought her carcase to me, and the streets of Whitby did echo with the clamour of my weeping.

Siân staggered among the gravestones on the East Cliff at midnight, drunk as a skunk. An immense full moon worthy of Dracula's demon lovers lit her way — that, and a dinky plastic torch with faltering batteries.

'Where are you, you sick bastard ...' she muttered, sweeping the feeble ray of torchlight over the headstones.

Her mission, as far as she could have explained it if someone had collared her on her way out of the White Horse and Griffin, was revenge. Revenge on a man who would murder his own daughter for falling short of some hateful religious ideal. Revenge on Mack for being so sickeningly right about everything, for seeking out the soft underbelly of her own faith in human nature and injecting it with a lethal dose of cynicism. Revenge on Saint Hilda and all her kind for being so pathetically impotent to stop anything tragic happening to anyone ever. Revenge on the eternal, unfathomable badness of human beings. Revenge on the whole damn Godless universe for deciding she must die when, really, if it was all the same to whatever damn random cellular roulette decided these things, she would rather live.

Revenge on THOMAS PEIRSON, WHALER AND OIL MERCHANT, whose headstone tilted before her now. Husband of Catherine, father of Anne and Illegible. Poor illegible Mary: given the cold shoulder by her lover, butchered by her father, erased from her pathetic few inches of memorial stone by two centuries of North Sea winds. Siân knelt on the ground and attacked the grave-plot with a trowel.

VIOLATED! MYSTERY GHOULS STRIKE IN CHURCH-YARD, that's what the *Whitby Gazette* would say.

Drunk as she was, it took her almost no time to realise that her grand plan of digging up Peirson and flinging his bones into the sea was a non-starter. The combination of her fury and one small trowel was not sufficient to send voluminous cascades of earth flying skyward; she was barely penetrating the grassy top-soil.

With a cry of disgust, she abandoned the attempt; she even threw the incriminating trowel away — let the police trace her and arrest her if they had nothing better to do! Bumbling provincials! She lurched back onto the hundred and ninety-nine steps, and promptly fell over, grazing her palms and wrists.

AMPUTEE BREAKS NECK ON CHURCH STEPS. No, not that; anything but that.

She forced herself to sit down on a bench and breathe regularly. Ten breaths of sea air were probably equal in sobering power to one sip of coffee; she would inhale lungfuls of salty oxygen until she was capable of walking safely back to the hotel.

For several minutes she sat on the bench, breathing in and out, trying to brush the sharp grains of grit from her bloodied hands. All the while, she stared down at the stone landing on which generations of coffin-bearers had rested their burden one last time before proceeding to Saint Mary's churchyard. Her feet — foot — feet, shoes, whatever, damn it — were occupying the same space as hundreds, maybe thousands of Whitby's long-vanished dead.

'I promised you,' whispered a male voice at her shoulder. 'I promised I would carry you up here, didn't I? And here we are.'

All the hairs on Siân's body prickled up, and she turned her face into an eerie brightness that had flowed up the hundred and ninety-nine steps like a car's headlight on full beam. A man was bending at her side, a man with a translucent white head and torso. Right through his glowing skin, faintly but unmistakably, she could see the dark windows and tiled rooftops of the houses below.

Instinctively she swung at him with her fist, and he was gone.

It was midday the following day before Siân even considered attempting anything more ambitious than rinsing her mouth with water. Mostly she just lay in bed, watching the slow progress of a shaft of sunlight through the velux window; it started pale and diffuse, on the skirting boards at the far end of the room, then moved inch by inch along the floorboards, growing in intensity, gradually enveloping the table and the blue plastic bag. Had Siân been upright and praying instead of slumped and groaning, she might have been a Benedictine nun in a prayer cell, aware of nothing outside her cloister but the sun making its stately progress through the unseen heavens.

Mack and Hadrian would be waiting for her at the Mission soon, but there was no way she was going to be able to keep that appointment. They would have to try again tomorrow, perhaps, when she was back in the land of the living.

She wondered if she should phone the site supervisor, to explain her non-appearance at the dig. Politeness aside, it seemed a pointless gesture, since her absence was surely obvious to everyone, and what would she say, anyway? *I've got the 'flu.* Or how about, *I'm massively hung over.* Or, if she was feeling really confessional, she could say, *Maybe you should find a replacement for me now. I'm thinking of killing myself while I'm still well enough to manage it.* Siân lay very still, imagining herself walking to the callbox at the foot of Caedmon's Trod and speaking these words into the telephone receiver. Then she remembered it was Saturday. No one was expecting her to be anywhere in particular.

Except Mack and Hadrian.

She looked at the alarm clock. Half past twelve. Mack surely had better things to do than wait for her: she could sense in him that typically male combination of hunger for female companionship and impatience with women for wasting men's valuable time. Perhaps he would go so far as to wander up the church steps, hoping to run into her. Perhaps he would even pay £1.70 to look for her at the abbey. Or perhaps, contrary to her instincts, he was head-over-heels in love with her, and would wait in the Mission coffee lounge until it closed and the Christian ladies shooed him out into Haggersgate, a sad young man with only a dog for company.

All she knew was that she was relieved she'd never told him where she was staying. She needed a sanctum, even if it was a hotel room that smelled of booze.

Strangely, despite feeling that there were toxic fumes rising from her body and that she must breathe very shallowly to give the pain in her head all the skull-room it demanded, she was a lot less miserable than she'd expected to be today. She hadn't had any nightmares, for a start, unless you counted the hallucination on the summit of the hundred and ninety-nine steps. For the first time since her accident, she'd survived a night's sleep without being pursued or mutilated. The notion of a few hours of benign unconsciousness, so taken for granted by other humans when they laid their heads on a pillow, was a novelty for Siân, and she hoped it might happen to her again sometime.

The despair she'd felt last night, the extremity of disgust and disillusionment with human nature, seemed to have faded too. She felt purged, hollow and airy inside, as if everything she'd ever known was no longer stored there. Like an infant, she knew nothing much about anything, and must wait for some clues from the universe before she could make any judgement of what sort of world she was in.

It was the strangest feeling, but not unpleasant.

As the afternoon progressed, Siân got herself ready for going out. She washed her hair, dressed nicely, applied Band-Aids to the abrasions on her palms and wrists, even though she knew they'd peel away in no time. Setting off from the White Horse and Griffin at three-ish, she thought she might go to the East Cliff and throw herself off the edge, hopefully dying instantly on the Scaur below, but instead, she crossed the bridge to the West Side, walked to Springvale Medical Centre and asked to see a doctor.

'I thought you'd decided you never wanted to see me again,' said Mack, when he found her waiting for him in the Whitby Mission & Seafarer's Centre on Monday, forty-eight hours after their original appointment.

'Thanks for coming,' she said, choosing her words with care. 'It was bad of me not to show up on Friday. I really wasn't well enough, though.'

He scrutinised her face, clearly unable to decide whether he should respond as a doctor or a lover, torn as he was between voicing professional concern, and praising her feminine charms regardless of how ghastly she looked.

'You look very tired,' he said, after some deliberation. He himself was in the usual fine shape, though so immaculately groomed and blow-dried today that he reminded her of a male model. She pictured him doing the rounds of hospital wards, accompanied by more nurses than strictly required. Or what about when he graduated to private practice? Female patients would discover hitherto unsuspected talents for hypochondria, no doubt. 'And I have to say . . .' he told Siân hesitantly, 'your face is rather flushed.'

'Oh, I really am sick,' she assured him, dabbing at her cheeks with the cool back of one hand. 'It's under control, though. Nothing for you to worry about.'

They were sitting in the Mission's alternative coffee lounge, the one with the sign above the door saying, 'Customers wishing to smoke or accompanied by a pet please use this room'. Hadrian was snuffling and whining under the table, doing his best not to bark, beating his tail loudly against the floor and the table-legs, and laying his head repeatedly in Siân's lap, for her to pat. Despite the animal-friendly sign above the door, he was the only dog in the room just now, and flirting shamelessly. Mack seemed nervous, rolling a cigarette from a crackling plastic pouch of amber tobacco.

'I didn't know you smoked,' said Siân.

'I don't — much,' he replied, indicating, with a shrug of his eyebrows, the slightly hazy atmosphere created by the folk at the other tables. 'I just get the occasional urge, when there's a lot of it in the air.' A sly, disarming grin spread slowly on his face, as though he were the town's most respectable schoolboy caught puffing on a fag behind a rubbish bin. 'Not a very good example for a doctor to set, eh? But at least I don't smoke the mass-produced kind.'

'Your big moral stand,' she remarked drily.

The sparring between them was beginning again, only a few minutes after their reunion. Magnus relaxed visibly, perhaps taking heart from this — or perhaps it was the nicotine.

'I've missed you,' he said.

She licked her lips, opened her mouth to reply.

'Hush!' said Hadrian, his skull clunking against the underside of the table.

Mack lifted the tablecloth and peered underneath, half-amused, half-annoyed. 'Hadrian disgraced himself here on Saturday, you know that?' he said, grabbing at the animal's tail to force him to turn around. 'Whimpered the place down, didn'tcha, eh, boy? That's the last time I take *you* anywhere.'

'Rough!' retorted Hadrian, as softly as his canine vocal cords allowed.

Mack allowed the tablecloth to drop, and Hadrian

returned to Siân, only his tail showing, a thick plume of white plush sweeping the smoky air. The other diners, mainly elderly couples, were smiling and nudging each other; this dog was better than the telly.

'Are you hungry?' said Mack.

'The ladies are making some warm milk for me,' said Siân. 'They're going to bring it when it's ready.'

He stood up and walked to the main coffee lounge to study the menu. Siân knew perfectly well that nothing would be to his liking. He would, she predicted, come closest to considering the slabs of quiche, but then reject them because the choice of 'flavours' was described, in the Mission's bluff un-Londonesque fashion, as 'cheese & onion' and 'bacon & egg'.

While waiting for him to return, she alternated between stroking Hadrian and flipping the pages of *Streonshalh*, the Whitby Parish magazine. The hot news was the latest ecclesiastical Synod — not the one Saint Hilda hosted in 664, obviously, but a forthcoming one. There were advertisements for videos and colour laser copies, but also long articles about the merits of the alder tree and the willow-herb. Since last month, a startling number of parishioners had died — more females than males, too, despite the supposedly superior life expectancies of women. Four different funeral directors offered Siân their services.

On a positive note, a mixed-voice choir called the

Sleights Singers, founded in 1909, serenaded her thus: 'New lady-and-gentleman members always made welcome'. Sure it was quaint, but behind the quaintness she sensed the genuine tug of human welcome, a reminder that if she were to show up at a particular house in Sleights on a particular night, she could have new friends instantly, and start singing with them. Siân committed the address to memory. If she was still alive next Thursday between 7.15 and 9, maybe she'd drop in.

Mack ambled back to the table and sat down.

'Nothing for Magnuses?' said Siân, deadpan.

'Nothing for Magnuses,' he agreed. 'Look, I know you've been ill and everything, but have you had a chance to ... ah ...'

She pulled her *Star Wars* notebook out of her jacket and held it up to her mouth, enjoying the loudness of this silent action. Indeed, she was thinking that all the words they'd spoken up to now had been superfluous, an elaborate verbal game, and could have been replaced with a few decorous hand gestures.

'I've got the whole thing now,' she said. 'It's all done.'

A matronly woman came to the table and set a tall glass of warm milk in front of Siân. She also laid down a cold pasty wrapped in a paper napkin.

'Wow,' murmured Mack when she'd walked back to the kitchen. 'If you pay extra, do you get a plate?'

'I told her the customer wouldn't need one,' said

Siân, immediately conveying the pasty under the table, where Hadrian scoffed it noisily.

Mack squinted at her in bemusement. 'Were you *so* sure we'd come?'

'No, I wasn't,' she said, and took a careful sip of her milk while, at her feet, the dog went *gronff, snuffle, flupp* and so forth. 'But I liked the idea of giving Hadrian this treat so much, that I bought it for him and hoped it would happen. And it has.'

He frowned, as if her rationale were a mystic riddle too thorny — or too stickily sentimental — for him to wish to grasp.

'OK: read,' he said, motioning towards the notebook. 'Please.'

She leaned forward, and he did too, so their faces were close together, causing a murmur of gossip behind them. Siân delivered the testament of Thomas Peirson in a soft voice, softer still during the more sensational bits, pausing every few sentences for a sip of milk. When she reached the part where Mary's body had been fished out of the River Esk, and her father was weeping for all he was worth, Magnus shook his head in admiration.

'Wow,' he said. 'Thomas Peirson, take a bow. Hollywood awaits.'

'I don't think so,' said Siân. 'There's more. I did the final page and a half last night. It's going to disappoint you, Mack.'

She cleared her throat, and continued reading, in the same soft tone as before. But these were new words, words she had uncovered in the wee small hours, when her sober hand had wielded the knife for the final time and she had wept tears of pity onto the frail old paper.

Of the events that followed, I have not the time to write. This Confession must be hid in the earth while I have yet strength to bury it. I will say only, that our Mary's funeral was one of the grandest this town has ever seen. She had a coach, drawn by six coal-black horses, and a long train of mourners bearing torches, for in those days burials were done after dark. When we carried her up the Steps, she had servers all dressed in white, carrying a maiden's garland afore her coffin, with ribbons held by all her friends. The Vicar spoke with full sureness of her place in Heaven.

Now, in my own dying days, I know not if I shall meet my daughter again. If she be in Hell, I pray that God finds reason to send me there; if she be in Heaven, I beg His forgiveness. These last years, folk have taken to calling me Bible Thomas behind my back, for I have read the Scriptures more than most Clergie-men, and there are some who say, He should have been a Monk, & a host of Whales would be the happier for it! None can guess why I have studied the Holy Book so earnestly, leaving not a word of it unturned — but I must be certain that no case like mine was ever judged before!

Under the strict terms of Scripture, I broke no Commandment — this much I know. I can also be sure of one other thing: that if I had left my daughter even as I found her, with the powder of poison on her dead lips, and the name of her faithless lover writ on her belly, she should have been buried in unhallowed ground with a stake through her heart. Now she lies among the Blessed, and soon I shall join her. For how long? Only at the Last Trump shall we know.

You who find this; You who read this — Pray for her, I beg of you!

Thomas Peirson,

father and Christian, as best he could be.

Siân laid the notebook on the table, and drank the rest of her milk. Hadrian had settled down to sleep on her feet, his warm flank breathing against her left shin. Magnus was frowning even more than before, his dark eyebrows almost knitting together.

'I don't get it,' he said. 'Was she a vampire after all? This stake-through-the-heart business . . .'

'It's how they used to bury suicides,' said Siân. 'Mary killed herself, Mack. She was already dead when her dad found her.'

His frown only deepened. 'So . . .'

'So he did what he had to.'

'Slashed his own daughter's throat so she'd score a place in the correct patch of dirt?'

Siân picked up her empty glass and shifted it to

one side of the table, as if clearing the way for an embrace – or an arm wrestle.

'Magnus,' she said as calmly as she could, 'I'm starting to wonder if you have everything it takes to be a good doctor. Can't you see that for our man Thomas, defending his child with a bit of 21st-century sarcasm just wasn't an option? As a suicide, she'd've been an object of disgust and shame; instead, he managed to get her buried with love and respect. You can't blame him for that.'

Mack leaned back in his chair and ran his hands through his hair, flustered, it seemed, from the effort of understanding such rank idiocy.

'But . . . what difference does it make? God's not fooled, is he? If Mary killed herself, she goes to Hell, right?'

'Maybe Thomas was hoping God would turn a blind eye.' Siân winced at the ugly vehemence of the sound Mack interjected – something between a sneer and a snort. 'Please, Mack: just once, try to put yourself into the mind of a person who believes there's an afterlife and a loving and just God. Imagine the end of the world, when the last trumpet sounds and all the dead rise from their graves, all the millions of people who've ever lived. Imagine God looking down on Whitby, at Saint Mary's churchyard, and there, in amongst all the resurrected souls, there's Mary, standing hand in hand with her father and mother and sister, all of them blinking in the light, wondering what happens next. Imagine. God and Mary's eyes meet, and suddenly each of them remembers how she died. The door to eternal life is open, the other townsfolk are walking through, all the drunkards and the gossips and the men who broke women's hearts. But Mary hesitates, and her father puts his arms around her. Now, tell me, Mack. If *you* were God, what would you do?'

Magnus pouted, scarcely able to believe what she was asking him, discomfited by the shiny-eyed intentness of her stare. 'I wouldn't've taken the job in the first place,' he quipped. 'I would've told the Deity Registration Board to go shove it.'

He flashed a grin, a pleading sort of grin painfully at odds with his sweating forehead and haunted eyes. He was evidently hoping the wisecrack would break the tension and restore an atmosphere of warm banter, but that hope died in the chill between them.

'Well,' said Siân with a sigh. 'It's a good thing nobody asked you, then, isn't it?' And she folded the notebook back into her jacket.

Alarmed at the prospect of her preparing to leave, Mack searched for a re-entry point, a way to prolong if not redeem their conversation.

'The bit . . . the bit about Mary having her lover's name written on her belly is weird, isn't it? Do you think she may have been mentally ill?'

Siân rested her chin on her clasped hands, half-closed her eyes. 'I think she was very, very unhappy.'

'That's what I was getting at. Clinically depressed, if she'd been diagnosed today.'

'If you like.'

'Or maybe she'd found out she was pregnant?'

'With a little test kit from the pharmacy?'

'I'm sure they had ways of knowing, didn't they, in the 18th century?' He looked at her hopefully, as if to call attention to his willingness to concede the wisdom of past ages.

'I don't think Mary was pregnant,' said Siân. 'Or if she was, she wasn't aware of it. I think this William Agar fellow deflowered her, and then rejected her, and she couldn't cope with the loss of her honour.'

'Wow. That's so Victorian. Or Romantic. Or something.'

'We all need a sense of personal integrity, Mack,' she said, finally pulling her feet out from under Hadrian's sleeping body. 'These days more than ever. There's far more people committing suicide now than at any time in history. What have all those people lost, if not their honour?'

'Yeah, but come on . . . To link whether you live or die to being dumped by a boyfriend . . .'

'Oh, I don't know,' said Siân. 'Who we give ourselves to is very important, don't you think?'

'Oof,' came a voice from under the table.

Siân shifted in her chair, and started laughing —
ticklish, involuntary laughter. Her right leg, having
gone to sleep some time ago, was suddenly buzzing
with pins and needles; the lump in her thigh was
giving her hell; in fact, the only part of her that didn't
feel lousy was the part that was manufactured by
Russian technicians.

'Are you all right?' said Mack, smiling nervously,
keen to share the joke.

'No, I'm *not* all right,' she groaned, and giggled
again. To make matters worse, Hadrian had woken
up, and was pawing gently against the leg whose nerve-
endings were going berserk. 'Have you ever been
dead, Mack?'

'*What?*'

'Have you ever been clinically dead? You know, in
an accident, before they revive you.'

He shook his head, dumbfounded.

'*I* have,' she went on. 'And you know what? I saw
the light that people always talk about, the shining
light on the other side.'

Before he could stop himself, Mack blurted, 'Yes,
I've read a couple of investigations into that: it's
actually the brain's synapses flaring or something...'

This, for Siân, was quite enough, and she rose
from her seat.

'Sorry, Mack,' she said. 'I have to go now.'

*   *   *

A week later, when Siân had just been released from hospital, she walked gingerly up the hundred and ninety-nine steps to the abbey. The ruins were still standing, large as life, despite a summer storm that had damaged roofs and satellite dishes on Whitby's more modern buildings. Siân walked all the way around, making sure nothing was missing that hadn't been missing already, then stood for a minute in the shadow of the abbey's towering east front, enjoying the Gothic symmetry of the great tiers of lancet windows and the scarred perfection of the ancient stonework. Maybe God still had plans for this medieval skeleton after all.

When she wandered over to the dig and said hello, her fellow archaeologists treated her like a returning heroine, everyone downing tools to crowd around her. Even the lovey-dovey couple from Wales were distracted from their industrious serenity long enough to ask how she was getting on. To be honest, everyone seemed extravagantly relieved that she was upright and walking around. This surprised Siân; she'd told no-one she was going into hospital, only that she was ill and needed some time off work, but her colleagues made such a fuss of her, she could have been Lazarus. Perhaps, in those agonised last few days before she'd gone to the medical centre and burst into tears in the arms of a nurse, the fear of death had been showing on her face, naked and ghostly pale, for anyone to see.

Then again, perhaps the fear had been showing for years.

The site supervisor told her that a handsome young man had been asking after her every day. Siân took the news pensively, as if calling to mind a host of men who might possibly be the one, then enquired if this guy had a beautiful dog with him. More a miserable-looking, whiny sort of dog, was the reply.

Warmed by the brilliant afternoon sun, Siân walked down to Saint Mary's churchyard, to the very edge of the cliff. She could tell that some of the soil had crumbled away during the storm, and fallen off the headland to the rocks below. Erosion was nibbling at the East Cliff, a never-ending natural labour to equalise the disparity between land and water. With every clod of earth that fell into space, empty air encroached closer to the great community of graves. At some stage in the future, sometime between tomorrow and when the sun turned supernova, Thomas Peirson's remains, and the remains of his loved ones, would tumble down to the shore of the North Sea.

Siân walked back from the edge onto the firmer terrain, found the Peirson headstone, and stood staring at it. She swayed a little on her feet, dopey with painkillers and antibiotics and the lingering after-effects of anaesthetic. The marks on the ground where she'd hacked with her trowel were barely perceptible, like scratches from a dog's claws.

Suddenly, out of the corner of her eye, she glimpsed something hurtling towards her, but before she could brace herself against the impact, she was knocked reeling. She didn't quite fall, though, and her assailant wasn't a car — it was Hadrian, bouncing back from her torso like an oversized soft toy thrown in a tantrum. While she was staggering and wind-milling her arms, he danced around her and offered woofs of encouragement.

A man's deep voice shouted 'Hadrian, no!', just as Siân managed to steady herself against Thomas Peirson's headstone. Magnus leapt to her side, his hand extended, and she grasped hold of it, even though it wasn't strictly necessary now.

'Christ, I'm sorry . . . !' said Mack. They stood locked in an absurd handshake over the graveplot, he dressed like a corporate businessman, she all in black like a Goth — the modern kind. Hadrian was bouncing up and down between them, panting and snuffling, and although his manic behaviour was annoying at first, it gave them a convenient excuse to let each other go.

'Maybe he's desperate for exercise,' Siân suggested, fondling the dog's sumptuous flank with both hands. 'Have you given up running?' And she aimed a nod at Mack's classically formal suit, the trousers of which were the kind she could imagine the wearer fastidiously inspecting for evidence of dog-hair. The memory of this man plastered with a dark arrowhead of sweat, scantily-clad in T-shirt and shorts, was difficult for her to retrieve now, so faded had it become.

'It got a bit . . . unmanageable,' he said, jerking forward in an abortive attempt to assist her as, with a grunt of pain, Siân knelt next to Hadrian and started stroking the dog in earnest. 'Hadrian wouldn't run with me anymore, you see. He'd just shoot ahead like a missile. Totally out of control.'

'And this is what drove you to dress up like a sales executive for an insurance firm?'

But his appetite for sparring seemed to have deserted him; instead of firing off a witty rejoinder, he only winced.

'I've got a meeting today, a conference,' he explained, his already rather pained eye-contact with her faltering. 'In fact, I'm leaving. Leaving Whitby.'

'Oh yes?' she said, after only a moment's pause in her stroking. 'Going back to London?'

'Yes.'

'Research paper finished?'

'Yes.'

'Proved what you wanted to?'

He shrugged and looked down towards the town, in the general direction of the railway station. 'That's for other researchers to decide.'

Siân had her arms around Hadrian's neck, her chin nudging his bony, downy skull. She waited a few more seconds to see if Mack would oblige her to ask, or if he'd have the courage to put her out of her suspense.

'What's going to happen to Hadrian?' she enquired at last, in the silence of the headland.

Mack blushed crimson, an ugly inflammation from the roots of his hair to the collar of his creamy-white shirt. 'I don't know. I'll take him with me, I suppose, but . . . I can't see myself being able to manage him in central London.' Sweat glistened on his great blushing forehead, and he began to stammer. 'Still, he . . . he's a pure-bred, isn't he, and I'm sure he's worth a mint, so I expect there'll be . . . experts, you know, connoisseurs, who'd . . . ah . . . take him.'

'How much do you want for him?' said Siân. She'd no doubt he would respond badly to this overture; braced herself for a shame-faced display of something horrible — craven retaliation, evasion, anger. She was wrong. He was enormously, unmistakably relieved.

'Siân,' he declared, clapping a palm to his brow, 'if you want him, you can *have* him.'

'Don't be silly,' she said. 'He's worth a mint, as you so . . . *bluntly* put it. How much do you want?'

Magnus smiled, shaking his head. 'I've owned him long enough, Siân. Now I want *you* to have him as a gift

— like those history books you dropped through my letterbox.'

'Don't be patronising.'

'No, no!' he protested, as animated and confident now as she'd ever seen him. 'You don't understand — I was thinking of offering for ages! It's just that I . . . I didn't know where you lived — whether you'd be able to have a dog there. I had an idea you might be staying in a hotel . . .'

'I might be,' she said. 'But I could move somewhere else, if I wanted to. If there was a reason to.' *Yes, Yes, Yes*, she was thinking, hiding her daft grin of exultation inside the dark fur of Hadrian's back. *Mine, Mine, Mine*.

'I just don't want you to be left,' Magnus was saying, 'with the wrong impression of me, that's all. Like I didn't have a generous bone in my body . . .'

She giggled, hugging Hadrian tighter to keep a grip on her own hysteria, her own longing to weep and wail. The wound in her thigh was throbbing; she wondered if it had burst its stitches when she was staggering off-balance.

'Don't want to go down in history misunderstood, eh?' she said.

With a flinch he acknowledged she'd scored a direct hit. 'Yeah.'

Siân stood up, using Hadrian as a four-legged prop, which the dog seemed to understand instinctively. She noticed Mack cast a furtive glance at his watch; only now did she twig that he probably had a train to catch, and a roomful of people somewhere in London waiting to be impressed by a man in an immaculate suit.

'I'm making you late, aren't I?'

'Nothing a few grovelling apologies to a bunch of medical registrars won't fix.' And he enclosed one giant hand gently inside the other, in an attitude of prayer, bowing his head like a penitent monk. 'Mea culpa, mea culpa.'

Time accelerated suddenly, as Siân realised this really was goodbye.

'I'll have to return your confession,' she said. 'And the bottle. Not through your letterbox, though.'

'Don't worry about it,' he said wearily. 'Keep it.'

'It's worth a hell of a lot more than a Finnish Lapphund, you do realise that, don't you?'

Her attempt to speak his language missed its mark; he smiled ruefully and looked away. 'Not to me. I liked it the way it was, before . . . before I understood it. When it was a mystery, a mysterious object my dad rescued from the ruins of Tin Ghaut when he was a kid. Something he'd take out to show me if I was good, and then put back in its special place.'

'I'm sorry, Mack,' said Siân. 'Mea culpa.'

'It's OK,' he said breezily. 'I'm sure you'll write an academic paper on it one of these days. Then you can thank me in the acknowledgements, eh?'

She stepped forward and embraced him, pressing her hands hard against his back. He responded decorously at first, then allowed himself to clasp her tight, uttering a deep and protracted sigh. He smelled of toothpaste, deodorant, aftershave and, very faintly, mothballs — a combination which somehow got past her defences and, despite her vow to avoid a melo-drama, made her cry after all.

'I don't even know your surname,' she said.

He groaned, and a hiccup of laughter passed through his breast into hers. 'Boyle.'

'Can't blame your father for that.'

'And yours?'

She hugged him tighter, suppressing a tiny fear, left over from the nightmares, that his hand would cease stroking her hair and seize her by the throat. 'It's a secret,' she said, and, pulling his head down to her lips, she whispered it in his ear.

When Mack was gone, Siân took shelter behind Thomas Peirson's gravestone and lifted her skirts to inspect her bandaged thigh. The gauze was clean and white, wholly devoid of the spreading stigma of blood she'd envisioned. Over-active imagination, as always.

Tentatively, she prodded the site of the surgery; it hurt less than before, and the pain was localised now, no longer a web of soreness throughout her innermost parts.

'It seems you've been carrying a little chunk of Bosnia around with you for quite a few years,' the doctor had said, when the X-rays were ready. She'd been slow to catch on, assumed he was making some smug, oh-so-penetrating comment about her relationship with the past. All he meant was that a fragment of stone, ploughed deep into her flesh when the car was dragging her mangled body twenty yards across a street roughened by tanks, had managed to escape detection in the desperate attempts to mend her afterwards. Overworked military surgeons saved her life, did their damnedest to save her knee, were forced by monstrous swelling and infection to sacrifice it. Somehow, though, in all the drama, an embedded crumb of tarmac had been overlooked, and had spent all these years since, inching its way — millimetring its way, more like — to the surface.

'That's not possible, surely?' Siân had said. But her conviction that she must be the eighth wonder of the world was gently undermined by medical statistics. The tendency of foreign objects to work their way out of people's bodies had been recorded, the doctor assured her, as far back as the Renaissance; there was, historically speaking, a lot of it about.

Siân stood at the top of the hundred and ninety-nine steps, fingering the morsel of rubble in her pocket, wondering if Magnus, running at the top speed that his suit and stiff black shoes allowed, had reached the railway station yet. She wondered how much older he might need to be, how much he might need to live through, before Time weathered him into the right man for her — counselling herself that he was sure to have found somebody else by then. The stone in her pocket was smooth as a pebble, as if her flesh had sucked it like a toffee for years, hoping to digest it. Over-active imagination again.

How odd to think that Whitby's sleepy harbour was twinkling here below her, obscured by a mushroom proliferation of typically English rooftops, while nestled inside her palm was a relic of a war-torn Balkan street thousands of miles away. She considered tossing it down the steps, just to see how long she could keep her eye on it before it became, irreclaimably, part of the British landscape. But, on balance, she preferred her original idea of getting a jeweller to fashion it into a pendant. A silver chain would be nice; Saint Hilda would have to forgive her.

She reached the abbey just as the last of the day's visitors were leaving. Homeward-bound American tourists looked at her in pity as she made her way towards the ruins; she wondered why, then realised they must think she'd just arrived on a late-running coach and was only going to get five minutes' worth of antiquity before being evicted by the English Heritage folks.

She walked to the sacristy and found the stone rectangle where Bobby and Jemima had shown off their superstitious spinning game. The vaguely human-shaped depression in the stone was, she had to admit, very inviting to lie in, even though its grey austerity had been tarnished by the words 'I WAS HERE' graffiti'd in yellow felt-tip. Tomorrow, with pious diligence, those words would no doubt be erased.

Siân looked right and left, to confirm that the tourists were all gone, and then she balanced herself carefully on one foot and, after a deep breath, began to spin. Her intention was to spin thirty-four times, but physicalities got the better of ritual and she found herself deliriously dizzy after only ten. With the land and sky revolving before her eyes, she laid herself down in the stone hollow, settling her shoulders and head in the proper place. For what seemed like ages, the turrets and piers of the abbey moved to and fro on the turf of the East Cliff like giant sailing ships made of rock, then finally glided to a standstill. Up there on the buttresses, the ghostie woman not only failed to jump, but failed to appear.

Siân gasped in surprise as her cheek was touched by something rough and wet and rather disgusting; Hadrian was licking her. She opened her mouth to scold him, but his preposterous name stuck in her throat.

'I think I'll call you Hush,' she said, elbowing herself up a little.

'Hush,' he agreed, nudging her to get to her feet.